THE BONE EATER

MARTY CHAN

thistledown press

No part of this publication may be reproduced or transmitted in any form or by any means, graphic, electronic or mechanical, including photocopying, recording, or any information storage and retrieval system, without permission in writing from the publisher or a licence from The Canadian Copyright Licensing Agency (Access Copyright). For an Access Copyright licence, visit www.accesscopyright.ca or call toll free to 1-800-893-5777.

Thistledown Press Ltd.
118 - 20th Street West
Saskatoon, SK   S7M 0W6

Library and Archives Canada Cataloguing in Publication

Chan, Marty, author
Barnabas bigfoot : the bone eater / Marty Chan.
(The Barnabas Bigfoot series ; book 3)

ISBN 978-1-927068-43-4 (pbk.)
I. Title. II. Title: Bone eater.

PS8555.H39244B38 2013   jC813'.54   C2013-903931-7

Cover illustration by Derek Mah
Book design by Jackie Forrie
Printed and bound in Canada

Canada Council   Conseil des Arts
for the Arts   du Canada

SASKATCHEWAN
ARTS BOARD

Canadian   Patrimoine
Heritage   canadien

We gratefully acknowledge the support of the Canada Council for the Arts, the Saskatchewan Arts Board, and the Government of Canada through the Canada Book Fund for our publishing program.

Acknowledgements

Thank you to the Alberta Foundation for the Arts, James Tapankov & the tech challenge students in the Pembina Hills District, Thistledown Press, Diane Tucker, Derek Mah, Michelle Chan, Marissa Kochanski, Wei Wong, and the Edmonton Public Library.

CHAPTER ONE

"We have to get out before they come back!" I said, my back hair bristling as I scanned the woods for movement. Something massive had crashed through the site, destroyed the camp and chased off the hunters. But if I knew anything about baldfaces, they wouldn't be gone for long.

Hannah chewed on the braided rat-tail of hair hanging from her neck. She glanced at her sister, trapped under the debris of what used to be a truck. Ruth's arm bent at an odd angle, and her full brown beard stuck straight out, a sign she was in pain.

"Hannah! Did you hear me? We have to free her before the baldfaces come back."

She snapped out of her daze and spat out her blond rat-tail. "Sour berries. Yes, I heard you. Ruth, can you move?"

Her sister groaned, "My arm is broken, but I think I can walk."

Hannah and I set to work, freeing Ruth from the wreckage. The baldface camp was a hairy tangle, much like my life. Many moons ago I was a sasquatch gathering nuts, roots, and berries for winter, but that changed when the baldfaces showed up.

These two-legged beasts rode smoky machines that choked out the air with what Grandma Bertha called "pull-ution," because the burning feeling the smoke created made her want to pull her throat out. The hunters trampled the forest's shrubs and flowers in their search for sasquatches. A group of them had captured me and took me away from my mountain home. A cruel baldface wanted to rip out my hair to cure baldness in his kind. I would have been lost forever if not for a baldface girl who helped me return home.

When I got back, I learned my troubles had only begun. More baldfaces were crashing around the woods in search of my tribe, and they had nabbed Hannah Hairyson. I followed her to a faraway island and, with the help of a baldface named Lysander, I rescued Hannah from a creature collector named Mr. Roland. Now that we had returned to the mountains, we were in a hairy tangle: all because of a traitor sasquatch named Dogger Dogwood. But as I looked at the wreckage around us, I realized we faced an even knottier tangle.

Broken perma-ice and twisted bars were scattered across the ground like autumn leaves after a windstorm. The only thing left standing was a giant perma-ice cage big enough to house at least six sasquatches. The giant box loomed over the flattened debris. This cage must have been well built to have survived the furious attack that had levelled the rest of the camp.

"You're going to be fine, Ruth," Hannah said. "Groom your hair. We'll have you out in a squirrel-tail shake. Barnabas, don't just stand there."

I helped Hannah. Together, we hefted a heavy panel of white wood off her sister. It crashed on the ground, setting off a round of twitter-chirps from chickadees in a nearby tree. My brown-haired friend rolled to one side and winced, clutching her broken arm. She shook her head, gritting her yellow teeth as her beard flared out again.

"Great mossy rock, my arm hurts," Ruth said, moaning.

Hannah rushed to her sister's side. Her moustache pointed straight out from both sides of her nose, a sign she was frazzled. She nervously stroked her moustache, trying not to let Ruth see how much the hair stood out.

"I'll take care of you. I'm here now. I'm here."

"Ow! Hannah. Stop touching my arm."

"We have to keep her arm steady," I said, recalling how Mom had tied branches on either side of Dad's leg when he had broken it many moons ago. "We need vines and something straight and stiff."

She backed off from her sister and stood up, her blond beard catching the afternoon sunlight, and headed off to the woods. Ruth nodded thanks to me. I smiled at her, then combed the nearby area for anything to help splint her arm. A few strides over, I found some yellow vines, which the baldfaces often used to tie things down. Hannah returned a few breaths later carrying two straight branches in one hand and a bright green bag in her other hand.

"What's that?" I asked.

She sheepishly held the bag up so I could smell. Inside was the dried soil we called delicious dirt but the baldfaces called coffee. They poured the stuff into hot water to make a drink. On one of the sisters' treks to the camps, they had discovered the delicious dirt. They loved the taste, comparing it to the bittersweet cedar bark they sometimes found in the valley. This coffee gave the sisters endless energy.

"I thought this might cheer her up," Hannah said.

"Delicious dirt! You are the best sister," Ruth said.

Hannah poured a handful of the loose soil into her hand and fed her sister. I knelt on the other side of Ruth as she closed her eyes and let out a happy sigh.

"This might hurt a little," I said as I placed the branches on either side of her arm.

"Do it fast," she said.

I wrapped the yellow vine around her arm, using the two splints to keep her arm straight.

She howled when I tightened the vine around her wrist.

"Great mossy rock, that *hurts*!" she yelped.

Hannah stroked her sister's brown beard. "You're going to be all right. Shh, shh. Do you want more delicious dirt?"

Even the promise of the treat did nothing to distract Ruth, who yowled and pulled away from me. I held her still and wrapped the vine around her splinted arm. Hannah hummed a sasquatch song to calm her down: "Winds blow strong, but not for long. The sun will rise and brighten your skies."

"Ow! Ow! Great mossy rock." Ruth's groans drowned out her sister's soothing song.

"Tell us what happened," I said, trying to take her mind off the pain.

She gritted her teeth and explained, "I'm not sure what happened exactly. I was heading up the mountain, sniffing for the tribe. I hoped to get to them before Dogger Dogwood and his clan did. I should have been paying closer attention to where I was walking, but I wasn't. The baldfaces had set a trap."

"Like the web that got me?" Hannah asked.

Hannah had been the first to land in a baldface snare, but Ruth and I had saved her. We learned later to watch out for vines tied around trees and for huge webs on the ground.

Ruth shook her head. "No, they shot me with these tiny arrows. Before I could run four or five strides, my head felt like a heavy stone and my legs became ice. I've never felt anything like that before."

"Hairy armpits. I have," I said, remembering the time the baldfaces shot me with a sleeping arrow.

"Me, too." Hannah added. "Did you get really tired?"

"Yes; I couldn't take another step without yawning. I took two, maybe three steps before I fell to the ground and went to sleep. When I woke up, my tongue felt like I had licked an anthill, and I was strapped down to a table in a chamber. A baldface had a silver circle attached to what looked like a black snake that split in two and nested in both his ears. He pressed the silver circle on my chest. It was so cold I wanted to scream."

"You didn't say anything, did you?" I asked.

She shook her head. "I was too scared. The baldface kept moving the circle around my chest. He talked to himself about how I was worth a big reward."

Hannah and I glanced at each other. "It has to be one of Mr. Roland's hunters," I said.

She nodded, then turned to her sister. "What else did he say?"

"Nothing. The next things I heard were shouts from outside. The baldface ran out of the chamber. Through the opening I could see, not much, but some things, like baldfaces running around. Then I smelled something powerful; like a sasquatch and a wolf, but much stronger. The baldfaces yelled at each other to shoot. At first, I thought our tribe was attacking the camp, but I didn't think Dogger Dogwood had the chest hair to lead a charge."

Hannah said, "If he ate pine cones, he'd be a squirrel."

"What else did you see?" I asked.

"There wasn't much light outside, except from the full moon, but I thought I saw a giant machine tossed through the air like a pebble thrown in a pond. The baldfaces yelled at each other to run away."

"Did you see the attacker?" Hannah asked.

She nodded. "A creature walked past the opening. The beast was covered in black hair, but it was no sasquatch. I've never seen anything so big. As big as eight black bears standing on each other's backs. The creature shredded one of the rolling caves faster than Mom strips leaves off a branch. The attack reminded me of the stories Dad used to tell about the Bone Eater. I thought they were stories, but last night I knew they were true. I could hear the beast pounding on something."

"It must have been trying to smash the cage," I nodded to the giant box that was still standing. "Why?"

"I don't know. Everything turned upside down. I hit my head and passed out. Then I woke up and you two were standing over me."

Hannah nibbled on the rat-tail of her blond hair. "Sour berries, if the Bone Eater is here, it won't be long before she finds the tribe."

I nodded. "We have to warn them."

"But that thing is in the woods. How are we going to get around it?" Ruth asked.

"We'll be safe during the day," I said. I finished tying the last knot in the vine. Her arm was set. "Done. How does that feel?"

She glanced down at her arm, set between the two branches. She gingerly moved it to one side, wincing in pain. Hannah helped her hold her arm steady while stroking the hair on her sister's back.

"Ow, ow."

"Easy, sister. Groom your hair."

Ruth eased her arm up and down. "It hurts whenever I move my arm."

"Then don't move your arm," I said.

"Don't be such a wise owl," she replied, narrowing her eyes.

Hannah, on the other hand, chuckled at my joke. She covered her mouth when her sister glared at her.

On the ground nearby, I noticed one of the baldface hides, a red and black top. I picked it up and tied the arms together. Then I wrapped the hide around Ruth's neck and made a sling for her broken arm.

"Better?" Hannah asked.

She nodded. "It'll do."

Her sister's moustache finally drooped as she relaxed. Still, Hannah hovered near Ruth like a bee looking for pollen in a flower.

"Tell me more about the Bone Eater. What is it?" Ruth asked as she adjusted the hide around her neck.

Hannah shook her head. "It's not an it. It's a *she*, and we met someone who knew her."

"What? Who? How? Where have you two been?" Ruth buzzed us with questions like a black fly.

"We'll explain on the way. Right now, we have to find the tribe," I said.

"If we're going to come across the Bone Eater, I don't want to be caught with my hair down," Hannah said, stooping over to pick up a metal bar.

"Not a bad idea," Ruth said, grabbing the bar with her good arm.

"Sour berries, I saw it first," Hannah said.

"You'd make me look for another weapon when I'm hurt? Ow, ow, ow," Ruth said, as she played up her injured arm.

"Fine, fine. You can keep it," Hannah grumbled. She went in search of another weapon. Meanwhile, I glanced down and noticed my foot-hides. Most of my body had filled out the way a growing sasquatch's body should. Most. My feet remained small, too small to belong to a member of the Bigfoot clan and too tiny to bear my weight. My parents said I was a late bloomer and my feet would eventually grow, but Grandma Bertha worried this might be a bad sign. She was right.

With a name like Bigfoot, the tribe members expected me to not only have the largest feet, but to also follow in the footsteps of my mother, her mother, and her mother's father, who were all tribe leaders. While sasquatches chose their leader, the responsibility always seemed to fall on the sasquatch with the largest feet, who usually happened to be a Bigfoot. The other tribe members expected me to take over when my mother stepped down. Worried about how I'd be treated by the other sasquatches, my parents made a pair of fake feet out of sasquatch hair and baldface foot-hides to disguise my secret. Now the white foot-hides were wearing out and the fake hair was falling off.

The sisters knew about my small feet — they were the only ones outside my family who knew — but I still felt like a bald patch when anyone looked at my real feet. As I backed away, I stepped on the butt of one of the baldface rifles. I picked it up by the barrel. It would make a good club, I thought.

"Let's go," I said. "Which way do you think the tribe went, Ruth?"

She grunted and led the way toward the edge of camp. I fell in line behind Hannah and followed Ruth into the woods. I took one last look at the wreckage. The perma-ice cage that stood in the middle of the debris looked like the snowcap on a mountain — a mountain that had suffered the Bone Eater's avalanche. I turned around and followed the sisters.

As we trekked through the firs and hemlocks, Hannah told her sister about how the creature collector Mr. Roland and his hunters had nabbed her. He gathered different creatures on his island and boasted he would add her to his collection. She was trapped in a cage like the giant one we'd left behind in the camp.

"How did you escape?" Ruth asked.

"Barnabas followed me."

I interrupted, "But I wasn't the one who saved her. Lysander figured out where the key to the cage was kept."

"Who's Lysander?" Ruth asked.

Hannah explained, "A baldface who helped us get off the island."

"Why would a baldface do that?"

I jumped in. "He owed our tribe for helping him."

Ruth's eyebrows knitted together like two rams locking horns. "Did you smack your head on a low-hanging branch? You expect me to believe that a baldface helped you?"

"Do you remember the story of the baldface who taught us how to speak the baldface language?" I asked.

She nodded.

"Well, Lysander is that baldface."

"You're yanking my hair. That story is older than great grandmother Laurel. This is like when Dad tried to tell us the strange whistle chirps from the mountains were from creatures trapped under the rock."

"He's telling the truth," Hannah said. "Our tribe rescued Lysander from baldfaces trying to kill him."

"How can he still be alive now?"

Hannah started to explain, but I shushed her. Off to the right, a few hundred strides away, I had heard a loud snap. We ducked. Silence. I lifted my head and sniffed the air. I detected the unmistakable scent of rotten lilacs and smoke. Baldfaces!

I pointed to the right. "Hunters. Fifty strides ahead of us," I whispered.

Ruth shook her head and pointed to the left. "They're thirty strides that way."

Hannah shook her head. "No, I'm picking up their scent to the right about twenty strides."

The truth dawned on me. We turned to each other, our back hair bristling with fear. We were surrounded.

CHAPTER TWO

R uth moved back, cradling her broken arm, until she stood even with Hannah and me. We scanned the fir trees, trying to spot the baldfaces in hiding, but while we could smell them, we couldn't see them. They were too well-hidden.

She motioned us closer.

"I recognize the scent of the baldface that was using the silver circle on me," she whispered.

"Mr. Roland's hunters must not want to give up the reward that easily," I said.

"Well they're not going to get Ruth again," Hannah said.

I shifted on to my knees and sniffed the air. The rotting lilac scent grew stronger. The baldfaces were moving in.

"Let's move back the way we came," Ruth suggested.

Her sister sniffed the air and shook her head. "They've moved in behind us."

Ahead of us, past a grove of firs, was a bluff. I couldn't smell any baldfaces at the top of the bluff and pointed at it. Hannah smiled, baring her yellow teeth.

Ruth shook her head. "Great mossy rock, the slope is too steep. I can't climb up with this broken arm."

"Maybe I can lead them on a chase away from you two," I suggested. "Hannah, you can help your sister up the slope and I'll catch up with you later."

She shook her head. "One of us always gets caught when we split up. We should stick together."

I shuddered at the memory of waking up in the perma-ice cage with a baldface leering at me. Hannah was right. If we were all going to get out of here safely, we'd have to work together. The problem was the baldfaces surrounded us. They crunched through the woods, getting closer.

"Get up," I ordered the sisters. "Follow me, but stay low."

I moved forward and headed toward the grove of trees, slipping from tree to tree, half expecting a sleeping arrow to hit me in the back at any breath. When I reached the fifth tree and no attack came, I relaxed. The noise behind us grew louder, but I couldn't hear anything to the left. I sniffed the air. There was only one baldface in that direction. I crept ahead, waving to the sisters to follow.

"They left an opening," I whispered. "They must not have enough hunters to surround us. There's only one this way. If we get by him, we'll be safe."

Hannah smiled. "Sweet cherries, something is finally going our way."

Ruth gritted her teeth whenever she brushed against the trunk of a tree or adjusted her balance. She refused to say she was hurting, but her brown beard flared out. I slowed down to give her a chance to catch her breath. The baldfaces' rotting lilac scent grew stronger. No turning back now. I didn't know what lay ahead of us, but we had to keep going.

The hunters picked up the pace. Their sounds grew closer. We wove our way through the trees. Our long legs gave us the edge as we easily stepped over the thick underbrush. We didn't need to follow a beaten path to move quickly through the forest, while the short-legged baldfaces would have to either chop through the brush or find another way.

The baldfaces must have sensed this, because they trampled through the woods faster and louder and shouted to each other: "Keep an eye out for the hairy beasts. If you see anything, call out."

I smiled as I walked, leading the sisters away from the hunters. Ahead, the lack of rotting lilac smell meant freedom. We were almost clear. Almost out of the clutches of the noisy baldfaces. Almost. I stopped short, raising my hand to stop the sisters.

"Keep going, Barnabas," Ruth hissed. "They're catching up."

"What's wrong?" Hannah asked.

"Do you remember Mr. Roland's island?"

She nodded. "What about it?"

"Remember how the baldfaces beat the bushes to herd us into a trap?"

"Do you want to swap stories after we get away?" Ruth said, her moustache sticking out to both sides.

"Hannah, does this seem familiar?" I asked.

She pulled her rat-tail from behind her head and chewed on it nervously. "Yes."

"What are you two talking about?" Ruth asked, her back hair standing straight up.

"Groom your hair, Ruth," I said, trying to calm her down.

Hannah shushed her sister. "Might be a trap."

"I'm going to check out why they want us to go this way," I said.

I scrambled away, careful about where I stepped. I tried to keep an eye open for any web traps on the ground, but the brush was too heavy. Instead, I looked from tree to tree for any of the black or yellow vines the baldfaces used to rig their traps. Branches had been snapped off along my path, as if someone had already been here. I lifted a green frond. Underneath was a baldface footprint.

I scanned the area. More branches had been snapped off along the path. The fir branches rested on the forest floor ahead of me like a blanket of green. Maybe the baldfaces used the branches as kindling to start a fire, but the way the branches lay across the ground, I thought this was either going to be a huge fire or the baldfaces had covered something up.

I swept my hand across the ground until I found a large rock. I lobbed it on to the blanket of fir branches and the rock fell through them, landing with a dull thud far below. Hairy armpits! A trap. I backed away, eyeing the area for any other dangers. After a dozen strides, I turned around and raced back to the Hairysons, but they were already running to join me. The sounds of the hunters grew louder.

Hannah panted. "They're coming after us. We have to go."

"This way," I said, moving to the right.

The sisters followed, but even before we ran ten strides, baldfaces appeared ahead of us. They yelled, "Got them! They're over here. Shoot them!"

I waved at the sisters to go back. A sleeping arrow struck the tree next to my head. I ducked and ran through the woods, overtaking the sisters as we headed in the opposite direction. More baldfaces shouted in front. The only way we could move was toward the pit trap. I motioned for Hannah and Ruth to meet me next to a wide pine tree. I told them about the trap ahead. Ruth gnashed her yellow teeth. Hannah chewed her rat-tail.

"We're going to be all right," I said. "We can go up." I pointed my rifle at the overhead branches, which would provide perfect cover if we could get high enough.

Ruth shook her head. "I can't climb. My arm. You two go."

"I'm not leaving you," Hannah said.

"Maybe we can haul her up," I suggested.

"With what? Barnabas, you'll need both your hands to hold on to the tree. You can't pull me up as well. Ow." She nursed her arm against her chest. The yellow vine around her wrist was digging in and she tried to loosen it. Hairy armpits! There was a way to unravel our hairy tangle. I dropped the rifle.

"Hannah, climb up the tree. Ruth, let me see your arm."

She gingerly eased her arm out of the red and black sling and held it up with her other hand, while her sister dug her fingers into the grooves in the tree and began to climb. Around us, the baldfaces crashed through the brush, moving closer. Judging by their shouts, I knew they hadn't found us yet, but if we didn't move fast, they'd be right on top of us. I untied the yellow vine and strung it out.

"Hannah, when you reach the first branch, let me know."

"Almost there."

"I just hope the vine is long enough," I said.

"For what?" Ruth asked.

"We're going to use it to haul you up the tree."

Her moustache curled as she smiled, baring her sharp fangs. "You're a big-footed genius."

"Only if this works. Hannah, are you there yet?"

"Hold your hair. Give me another couple of breaths. Okay, I'm ready."

"Catch the vine," I ordered, then I tossed one end up. It plunged to the earth like a dead snake.

"Throw it higher," Hannah instructed.

I picked up the vine, coiled it, and then launched the whole thing up. It didn't fall back down.

"Toss me one end," I said.

The baldfaces sounded close.

"Hurry," Ruth hissed. "They're almost on top of us."

I watched as the yellow vine snaked down, but it stopped short of my reach. Even if I could jump up to get it, there wasn't going to be enough to tie around Ruth.

She eyed the dangling rope and then looked to the brush around us. "I think my good arm is strong enough to hang on. If you steady me from behind, this might work."

"Ruth, we can't even reach the vine."

"Not on our own. Bend over, Barnabas."

"Why?"

"Just do it," she ordered.

I stooped over. Ruth grabbed my shoulder and pushed me to my knees while she threw one of her hairy legs over my shoulder. Her plan became as clear as the stench of her feet. I placed one of my hands against the tree trunk to steady myself and used the other hand to steady Ruth as she climbed on my shoulders.

"Ugh," I grunted.

"I'm not that heavy," she said. "Stand up."

"Erg," I groaned as I pushed up. My legs shook from her full weight on my shoulders. Sweat ran down my forehead, rolling down my bare cheek. I had never felt sweat on my bare cheek before. I imagined a slug crawling down my face. I hated the sensation and longed for my facial hair to grow back.

More shouts from the baldfaces: "We're closing in! Close the circle, men!"

With one last mighty effort, I straightened my legs and stood up, bracing my hands against the tree trunk. I swayed to one side, trying to keep my balance on the fake foot hides. They were pretty beaten up. Wind rushed through holes and I could see the sasquatch hair was falling off. As I tried to get a better stance, my feet slipped inside the foot hides and I had to take a step to keep myself from falling over.

"Hold still," Ruth hissed.

"Hairy armpits," I said. "This isn't easy."

"You think I'm having fun?" she said, grimacing as she reached up to grab the vine with her good hand.

The dangling vine swung out of her reach. Once. Twice. Three times. Finally she snagged it and twirled her hand, wrapping the vine around her fingers.

"Pull," Ruth ordered her sister.

I could feel her lift up off my shoulders, but only by a few short hairs. Above us, Hannah pulled. I dug my fingers into the grooves of the trunk and started to climb, but my foot hides slipped against the smooth bark. I couldn't dig my toes into the grooves. There was no choice. I kicked off the foot hides. I dug my toes into the grooves and began to climb with Ruth on my shoulders.

The baldfaces sounded like they were right behind us. Against the bark of the tree, we might have blended in with our dark hair, but the yellow vine was a dead giveaway. We had to get to the upper branches.

"Keep pulling," I said, straining to hold the weight of Ruth as I climbed the tree.

Her knees bashed against the trunk, but she made no noise. She rested her broken arm on the top of my head. I glanced down. We were making progress, but it was like waiting for hair to grow. Only three arm's lengths to the protective cover of the upper branches.

"Over here!" a baldface yelled.

I flattened myself against the trunk. Ruth's weight settled on my shoulders. The vine went slack and I started to slide down the tree. Hairy armpits, we were caught.

CHAPTER THREE

The sounds of the baldfaces crashing through the brush grew louder. Ruth and I could do nothing. We were like a bald patch on a hairy back, visible to everyone. I closed my eyes and waited for a sleeping arrow to hit me. Above me, Ruth squeezed her thighs against my ears until it felt like my eyes were going to pop out of my head. Hannah grunted as she pulled on the vine.

"It's behind us!" the voice cried.

Another baldface shouted, "Don't lose it. Go, go, go!"

The sounds started to move away from the tree. I glanced down and saw the tops of the baldfaces' heads as they moved away from us. Something had attracted their attention. Maybe it was Dogger Dogwood coming to finish what he started, but I picked the lice of that thought out of my hair. If it were him, he didn't have to do anything except watch the baldfaces catch us. Whoever led the baldfaces away was on our side, but I couldn't spare the breath to wonder who it was.

"I don't know when they'll be back," I said. "We have to go now."

"Great mossy rock, take it easy, Barnabas," Ruth said. "My arm."

Hannah called down to us, "Hang on to the vine, Ruth. It'll take the weight off Barnabas."

Within three breaths, my tiny feet touched the cold moist ground. I lowered Ruth off my shoulders as Hannah hopped down. She scooped up the branches and wrapped the yellow vine around them.

"Did you see who led the hunters away, Hannah?" I asked.

"It looked like a sasquatch, but I couldn't see who."

"We can solve that mystery later," Ruth said. "I'd like to put a couple of mountains between us and the hunters."

"Give me a couple of breaths," I said. I rubbed my butt against the tree trunk.

"We don't have the breath to waste for you to mark your territory," Hannah said.

"Just in case we have to come back to this area, I want to know where the trap is."

"Let's go already," Ruth urged.

I stepped away from the tree, picked up my rifle and led the sisters away. My feet hurt as I stepped on roots and rocks along the slope. Without the fake foot hides as protection, my feet were at the hairy mercy of the forest. Other sasquatches like Ruth and Hannah toughened the soles of their feet over many winters, but my feet were as sensitive as a newborn sasquatchling's. This slowed me down as we reached rockier ground. I waved for the sisters to stop so we could set Ruth's arm, but secretly I needed to give my feet a break. I rubbed the soles, clearing away pine needles that had jammed between my toes.

Hannah unravelled the yellow vine and set the branches on either side of her sister's broken arm. I helped her tie the splint. Ruth gritted her teeth and muttered in pain.

"Sour berries," Hannah said, slapping her hand to her forehead.

"What?" I asked.

"The bag of delicious dirt broke open in the treetop." She brushed the brown crumbs from her body hair.

"That's the least of our worries," I said.

Ruth eyed her sister. "I could use some delicious dirt right now. It always perks me up."

Her sister licked delicious dirt off her finger. "Oops, that's the last of it."

"We could go back to the tree," Ruth suggested.

"We're not going back for delicious dirt," I said. "We have to find the tribe. Ruth, do you remember the last scent of their trail?"

She blocked the high sun out of her eyes and squinted around the mountain. Then she pointed at a valley. "There. They can't be far if they sent one of the tribe members to lure away the baldfaces."

Hannah nodded. "Maybe we should wait here for them to find us."

I disagreed. "Who knows what Dogger Dogwood and his clan have been telling everyone? The sooner we get there, the better. Let's go."

My feet howled in pain as I walked down the rocky trail, but I pushed forward. Behind me,

Hannah sniffed the air, making sure we weren't going to be caught in another ambush. Taking up the rear, Ruth adjusted the red and black baldface sling. Without my fake foot hides, it was harder to keep my balance and I had to use the rifle to steady myself. Once in a while, I had to catch myself against a tree trunk to keep from doing a face plant.

The further down the slope we travelled, the more difficult the terrain. At one point I had to kneel to steady myself between the Hairysons. Hannah suggested we go back for the foot hides, while Ruth told me to trade the rifle for a long branch. I ignored them both and hobbled ahead of them.

"I'm fine," I said. "I don't need the foot-hides. Let's just go."

I did a nose-first face plant into a shrub.

"Maybe we should rest here," Hannah offered. "Ruth looks like her arm's really hurting."

"I'm fine," her sister shot back.

"Ruth, you look like you could use some rest," Hannah said.

I noticed her nodding to her sister as she pointed at me.

"Oh yes, of course, my arm does feel sore. Let's stop," Ruth said.

I could handle the Hairysons' teasing, which stung like black fly bites: painful at first but soon fading away. But their pity stabbed me in the belly like never-ending hunger pangs. I fought the gnawing shame eating away at me by standing up and bracing myself on the baldface rifle. "Hairy armpits! We can't rest. Who knows if Dogger Dogwood will turn over another sasquatch to the baldfaces?"

Ruth shot back, "Don't you think I know that? I had nothing else to think about while the baldfaces held me."

"Then you know we have to move on."

"Don't you dare take that tone with me, Barnabas Bigfoot."

"What tone is that?" I asked.

"The one where you act like your hair never gets tangled."

"You're one to talk. You're always tossing pebbles in puddles just to get sasquatchlings wet."

"Enough," Hannah said. "This is no way for a tribe leader to act, Barnabas."

I fell silent, glaring at Ruth. She turned her hairy back on me. Hannah was right. I was the tribe leader now, at least until my mother and grandparents came back from their scouting mission. I had hoped my dad would rule the tribe while she was away, but he was gone. He had . . . no, now was not the right time to think about what had happened to him.

The responsibility for leading the tribe fell on the next Bigfoot family member until the tribe members selected a new leader. Hannah was right. If I was going to be a tribe leader, I had better start acting like one.

"I apologize, Ruth. My hair was out of place."

She grunted, but turned around and gave me a slight nod.

Hannah reached out and helped me stand. "What's our plan once we find the tribe, Barnabas?"

"Great mossy rock, it's simple. We tell the tribe to kick Dogger Dogwood and his clan out," Ruth said.

I shook my head. "We have to warn them about the Bone Eater first. The tribe is more in danger from her than Dogger Dogwood; at least until the full moon passes."

"How do you know?" Ruth asked. "What do you know about the creature?"

"Do you remember Lysander?"

"You mean the ancient baldface who lived with our ancestors?" she asked as she rolled her big brown eyes.

"Yes," I said, ignoring her hair-plucking comment. "What we didn't tell you was he's a lycanthrope."

"What's that?"

Hannah explained. "On a full-moon night, he turns into a wolf. Like when a caterpillar turns into a butterfly."

I added, "He called it *the change*."

"You can call it a sun, but that's not going to make it the truth," Ruth said.

"We're not lying, sister."

"When the tribe took him in, he was a wolf," I said, "but when the morning came, they found they had a baldface in their midst. That's when they learned that he was a lycanthrope."

"A baldface who can turn into a wolf. Yes, that's quite the *story*."

Hannah hushed her sister. "Let him finish."

"The reason Lysander left the tribe was because when he turned into a wolf, he was dangerous. He forgot who he was and who his friends were. He hid from the tribe on full moon nights so he could change into the wolf without hurting anyone, but one night he wasn't careful and he bit one of the tribe members."

"Daphne Dogwood," Hannah added.

"Yes, one of Dogger Dogwood's ancestors," I said.

Ruth twirled her moustache, gazing at us with narrow-eyed disbelief. "Go on."

"When a creature like Lysander bites another baldface, the baldface turns into a wolf like Lysander. But this was the first time he'd ever bitten a sasquatch."

"What happened to Daphne Dogwood?" Ruth asked.

"She became the Bone Eater."

She cracked a gap-toothed grin at me, then at Hannah. A snicker slipped past her lips, followed by a giggle. The giggle grew into snorts of laughter. "Hairy-larious," she said, slapping her knee.

"He's telling the truth," Hannah glared at her sister, who was now yipping with laughter.

"Sure, sure, I believe you two. And does the Bone Eater live on the moon when the moon's not full? Ha, ha, ha, ha, ha."

"Sour berries, what's so hard to believe, Ruth?"

"Everything, Hannah. Find me the low-hanging branch you hit your head on. It must have been a thick one."

"Believe what you want," I said, "but we have to protect the tribe from the Bone Eater."

Hannah grabbed her sister's good arm. "You saw what the beast did to the baldface camp."

This fact silenced Ruth's laughter. "I'm sorry, Hannah. Barnabas. You're right. I may not believe your story, but that doesn't change the fact that a monster is roaming the mountains. We need to warn the tribe."

"We're wasting breath standing here," I said. "We'll have a better chance of picking up the tribe's trail if we split up. I'll head down this way. You two fan out. We'll meet in the valley." I glanced at the sun, which was past its highest point. Half the day was gone. "We'd better hurry."

The sisters headed down the sloping mountain toward the valley, while I staggered from tree to tree, stopping to sniff the air for sasquatches. The loam was rich and earthy and there was the stray scent of a deer, a squirrel family, and an owl, but no sign of sasquatch, Bone Eater, or baldface. I wondered if I'd find the tribe before nightfall.

When I reached the valley, my worries turned out to be so much loose hair. A hundred strides ahead of me I picked up the scent of sasquatch mixed with chokecherries. It had to be Yolanda Yeti. She loved to eat the sour berries. She told everyone the berries made her breath fresh, which led to the sasquatch saying "fresh as a Yeti."

She was my mom's best friend. Mom had rescued Yolanda Yeti's clan during a snowstorm. If it weren't for my mom, the Yeti clan would have starved to death on an icy mountain many, many strides from our mountain home. For that, Yolanda Yeti promised her loyalty to the Bigfoots.

I picked up the pace, excited to tell her about Dogger Dogwood's betrayal. Yolanda Yeti was famous for her hairy fits. When she was angry, the hair on her back stiffened like porcupine quills and her growl made black bears scamper.

I couldn't wait for her to tear the hair off Dogger Dogwood's back for trying to hand us to the baldfaces. I found her sniffing around some bushes, picking the last of the fall berries.

I rushed forward, but there were no more trees to steady against and the rifle was too short. I fell forward, landing on my knees. Her beard stiffened and her bushy white eyebrows flared out like a skunk tail spraying.

"B . . . b . . . b . . . baldface," she stammered, backing up.

"No, it's me," I started to explain, but she turned and bolted away before I could say another word.

CHAPTER FOUR

I climbed to my feet and chased after Yolanda Yeti, but she had too much of a head start. I tripped over my feet before I could even get ten strides. I cursed my shaven face for scaring her off. Her chokecherry scent led me to the edge of the clearing. A few hundred strides into the woods, I picked up the scent of coffee. Hannah was close. I plopped onto a tree stump and waited for her, rubbing my sore feet. Blisters like giant mosquito bites had formed on my soles. The flesh around the bumps was hard and starting to crack. The blisters themselves throbbed every time I touched them.

Hannah strode through the underbrush, sweeping away low branches. She stopped a few strides away and sniffed the air, then broke into a wide yellow grin. "Fresh as a Yeti. Where is she?"

I lowered my feet and hooked them around the stump behind me so Hannah couldn't see the blisters. "She's near. Where's Ruth?"

"Behind you," Hannah said, pointing.

Ruth tromped through the woods, her arm wrapped in the baldface hide. I slid over so she could join me on the stump. She adjusted her sling.

"Sweet cherries, you did great, Barnabas," Hannah said. "You found the tribe before nightfall."

I shook my head and told them about Yolanda Yeti's reaction to my bare face. She had moved faster than a frightened hare.

"Once we explain who you are, she'll understand," Hannah said.

"They'll scatter as soon as they see my face," I said. "What kind of tribe leader scares his followers? We can't very well warn them about the Bone Eater if they're running away from me." I rubbed my cheek and stared down at the ground.

Ruth stared at me. "Barnabas has a point. Normally, his face gives us all a good reason to scream, but the first time I saw your bare face I was scared hairless. I can only imagine what the tribe will think when they see you."

"So what do we do?" Hannah asked.

I eyed the sky and the sun as it started to dip behind one of the snow-capped peaks. Night was coming. We couldn't wait any longer. "The best thing to do is for me to stay hidden. You have to go on your own and tell them what happened. I'll watch from a distance until you give me a signal that it's okay to join you."

"That's a good idea," Ruth said.

Hannah nodded.

I leaned against the rifle and pulled myself upright. "You two get going. I'll catch up."

The sisters hesitated.

"I can smell the delicious dirt on Hannah from a mountain range away. I'll be able to find you."

"Don't worry, Barnabas. By the time Ruth and I are done talking to the tribe, they'll welcome you with open arms. And if we're lucky, they'll string Dogger Dogwood up by the nose hairs."

The sisters set off after Yolanda Yeti. I hobbled after them. They were deep in the woods, but the unmistakable aroma of delicious dirt lingered in the air. I climbed out of the valley, moving up the slope of a mountain. About halfway up I picked up the scent of many sasquatches gathered together. I limped to a plateau and spotted the tribe. I climbed to the top of a hill and lay down to watch. The tribe members surrounded the sisters, but I was too far away to hear them. I scanned the group for the Dogwood clan, but I couldn't clearly see the features of the sasquatches. Nothing else to do but wait.

I backed down from the crest of the hill and sat up. Waiting for the Hairysons to convince the tribe, I felt like I was waiting for the lake ice to melt; it was taking longer than I wanted it to. To pass the time, I examined the rifle. The butt end felt like smooth wood covered in resin and the black barrel was made of a shiny metal. I was pretty sure the sleeping arrows came out of the hole at the end of the smooth barrel. A smaller black tube sat on top of the long barrel. Perma-ice covered either end. I wondered what the baldfaces kept inside this narrow black tube. I lifted the rifle so I could peek through one end.

My jaw dropped open. Through the tube, the trees seemed so close that I could reach out and touch them. When I looked at the trees without the tube, the trees stood far away. Somehow, this baldface tube brought objects closer, or at least made them appear that way. I smiled as an idea took shape. I crawled back to the top of the hill, set the rifle on the crest, and peered through the tube at the tribe. Sure enough, I saw them all as if I were standing next to them.

Hannah tried to calm down Yolanda Yeti, who gestured at her face and howled. I don't know what she was saying, but the way she pointed at her face, I guessed she was describing me. The next image that entered my field of vision curled my butt hair. Dogger Dogwood stepped into view and hugged the Hairyson sisters. He seemed pleased to see them. I couldn't see Hannah's and Ruth's parents. Where were Juniper and Hemlock Hairyson?

I swung the rifle back to the sisters. I went too far and spotted Delilah Dogwood and Dogger Dogwood's black-haired sons, Deacon and Darwin. They seemed angry, but no one noticed.

When I finally found the sisters again, they were glaring at Dogger Dogwood, who spoke to the tribe, gesturing wildly with his arms. Everyone gaped at him. I wondered if he was trying to talk his way out of this hairy tangle he had created for himself. Then something strange happened.

The sasquatches started to raise three fingers, the sasquatch sign for good job. Some patted Dogger Dogwood on the back. Others embraced Hannah and Ruth and stroked their hair. Then he waved his sons over and leaned in to talk to them. He preened his black hair, pulling his beard into an even point as he spoke. Darwin and Deacon nodded and then they left the group. Dogger Dogwood put an arm around each sister and led the Hairysons to the camp. Neither Ruth nor Hannah looked pleased.

I felt helpless on the crest of the hill. I had to find out what Dogger Dogwood had told the tribe, but I was too far away to hear anything. The Dogwood brothers, on the other foot, headed in my direction and I believed they would know the hairy strands of their father's lie. I looked up from the rifle and spied on the brothers striding toward the hill. I crawled along the ground to hide behind some bushes.

They walked past, unaware of me. As Grandma Bertha said, they had hair in their eyes. I crawled after them. Darwin stopped, grabbing his brother. I froze in my spot and listened.

"Did you hear something, Deacon?"

"Only your mouth breathing, brother." He tittered like an angry squirrel protecting her kittens.

"Pull the hair out of your ears," Darwin said. "We have to be careful."

"Bald patch, do you think Dad was right about the baldfaces being in the valley?"

Darwin smacked his brother across the back of the head. "Did you hit your head on a low-hanging branch? Dad told that story to scare the others. The baldfaces aren't anywhere near here."

"Then why did he say there might be some in the valley?" Deacon asked.

His brother sighed. "So when we go back and say we can't find the Hairysons, Dad can say the baldfaces got them. Pretty smart plan, eh?"

"Oh yes. Smart. Very smart. Really smart. Why is it so smart?"

"If Ruth and Hannah think their parents are in trouble, they'll be tied up in knots about whether or not to tell the tribe about what we did."

"Wow. Amazing. Hairy-riffic. Incredible."

"You still don't understand, do you?" Darwin asked.

"No. Not really."

"Sometimes I wonder if you're a true Dogwood. You're as dumb as a Bigfoot."

Deacon rose to his full height. "Take that back."

"Groom your hair. Dad's plan is simple. As long as Juniper Hairyson and Hemlock Hairyson don't come back, we can say anything happened to them — like the baldfaces captured them."

"But that won't be true when they come back to the camp."

Darwin narrowed his eyes at his brother. "That's why we're going to make sure they don't come back."

"How? You just said there are no baldfaces."

"We tie them up and leave them out here."

"Oh, now I get it," Deacon said. "Except, why did Dad tell us to bring them back to the camp?"

"Bald patch!" Darwin exploded. "It was a lie. Let me make this simple for you, Deacon. Do everything I tell you to do and keep your hairy mouth shut. Understand?"

No answer.

"I said do you understand?"

Still no answer.

"Pull the hair out of your ears, Deacon. I asked you a question."

"But you told me to keep my mouth shut."

Darwin's shoulders sagged. "Keep your mouth shut when we get back to camp."

"Oh, okay. For how long?"

"Never mind. Let's go. I want to find the Hairysons before we lose the sunlight."

Hairy armpits. Dogger Dogwood was a cowlick in a neat beard. I never expected how far he would go to save his own beard. This sasquatch had to be stopped, but to do that I needed allies; I needed to save the Hairysons from the Dogwood brothers. I stood up, braced myself with the rifle, and stumbled after the pair. I'd barely travelled twenty strides when something hard struck me in the back of the head. I reeled forward, dizzy from the blow, turning as I landed on my butt. I looked up at what had hit me. Not what, but who: Delilah Dogwood. In her hands, a thick branch.

Then everything went dark.

CHAPTER FIVE

My head felt like a mountain had landed on it. As I started to regain my senses, I heard voices around me. There was an argument going on about what to do with the baldface. I thought I heard Hannah calling for everyone to calm down and listen, but the sea of panicked cries to flee drowned her out. I opened one eye and found myself staring at the huge feet and hairy legs of the sasquatches around me. I tried to sit up but my arms and legs were bound. Instead, I rolled on to one side and suddenly all the voices stopped.

Every single sasquatch was now looking down at me. Their beards were all standing at attention and their prickly body hair gave off the scent of fear. Everyone backed away.

"It's hideous," Yolanda Yeti gasped.

"I always wondered what baldfaces hid under their hides," another sasquatch said. "I didn't know they had hair like us."

"He's not a baldface," Hannah defended, moving to the front of the crowd.

Ruth backed her up. "He's Barnabas. Barnabas Bigfoot."

The sasquatches examined me. Yolanda Yeti shook her head. "I'd recognize his hairy face anywhere, and that's not him."

"Trust me, he's a Bigfoot," Hannah explained.

"It's me," I croaked.

Yolanda Yeti stiffened. "It sounds like him, but his face . . . "

"Smell his armpits," Ruth said. "Then you'll know the truth."

The sasquatches looked to each other, nervous, plucking at their own hairs, waiting for someone to go first. Hannah knelt beside me and beckoned Yolanda Yeti to come closer. "He's Barnabas. He's one of us."

Finally, Yolanda Yeti inched forward, knelt down, and sniffed my armpit. She straightened up, looking down at me with wide owl eyes. "Barnabas?"

I nodded. "Yes. It's me."

She turned to the others. "He *is* Barnabas Bigfoot."

Murmurs of relief spread through the group as they moved closer. Yolanda Yeti reached out and touched my bare face, pulling her hand back and shuddering. "What happened to you?"

"I had to cut my hair to blend in with the baldfaces."

"Why did you want to do that?" she asked.

"It's a long story and we don't have time," I said. "The Bone Eater is coming!"

The sasquatches shifted nervously, as mutters spread through the group. Many of the sasquatches shook their heads. Some of the younger ones scoffed. "That's an old hairy tale used to scare sasquatchlings. There's no such thing."

But the older sasquatches tugged on their beards and glanced at each other.

"The Bone Eater is real and it's here," I said.

Everyone talked at once. Some of the older sasquatches moved closer to their children and put their arms around them, trying to hush their questions about whether or not the Bone

Eater was real. A few cast nervous glances at the woods.

Yolanda Yeti waved for silence. "Enough!" Then she scolded me. "Don't joke about the Bone Eater, Barnabas."

"He's not making it up," Ruth said. "I saw the creature myself. It crashed through a baldface camp."

"What were you doing there?" someone at the back asked.

Yolanda Yeti answered, "That's probably where the baldfaces took her when they captured her and Hannah."

Lorcan Longfoot, one of the most skitterish sasquatches in the tribe, pushed ahead and asked. "Were you in the camp, Barnabas? What do the baldfaces want to do to us?" He started to pull at his straggly brown arm hair as he chewed his bottom lip nervously. "Are they going to take our hair?"

I shook my head. "Listen to me, the problem isn't the baldfaces. We have to find a place to hide from the Bone Eater." I glanced at the sun, now starting to set.

"Yes," Ruth said, backing me up. "The creature is powerful. It turned over one of the rolling caves that I was in. That's how I broke my arm," she said.

The hushed whispers turned into a dull roar as every sasquatch argued about whether or not we were telling the truth.

"Please untie me," I asked. "I can explain everything."

Yolanda Yeti nodded and reached down to unbind my legs. However, before she could get to my arms, Dogger and Delilah Dogwood pushed through the group. "Don't you dare free that baldface," he howled.

"It's Barnabas," Yolanda Yeti explained. "I smelled his armpit."

Dogger Dogwood towered over me, grooming his long black neck hair and flashing his yellow teeth at the sasquatches around him. His sister crossed her arms and glared at me. I fired back with a fur-ocious stare, recalling how she had struck me with the branch. Dogger Dogwood raised his hand for silence, but the sasquatches continued to natter until his sister stuck her fingers in her mouth and whistled. This silenced everyone. She was probably the toughest and meanest sasquatch in the tribe. No one dared cross her. She nodded to her brother.

"Good sasquatches, listen to me. When I was a sasquatchling, I too feared the evil Bone Eater. The stories my father told me made my hair stand on end. I couldn't sleep for nights. Do you remember how I curled into a ball, sister?"

She grunted, "You were scared hairless, brother."

"And I'm sure I wasn't the only one. In fact, I remember my dear departed wife, Delora Dogwood, would tell our sons the same stories to make sure they didn't go into unknown territory by themselves. But they were just stories." He eyed the younger sasquatches, who nodded.

Yolanda Yeti argued, "There is always a knot of truth in any hairy story."

He nodded. "Yes, Yolanda Yeti, there is. And maybe one time, many, many, many winters ago, this Bone Eater roamed the mountains in search of sasquatch bones to chew, but we have not seen its like since. If it is as old as the legends, then the monster of the mountain is as old as the trees. Do you know of any beast that can live that long?"

Yolanda Yeti had no answer. The older sasquatches fell silent.

"Leave these stories to the sasquatchlings. We have a real threat before us, and that is the baldfaces."

"No!" I cried. "His lies are the threat. Tell them, Hannah. Ruth?" I looked to the sisters for help. They looked down at the ground.

"You mustn't upset the Hairysons. Don't worry, girls. I'm sure my sons will find your parents before the baldfaces do. They'll be safe."

I shook my head. "Sasquatches, you can't trust anything Dogger Dogwood says. He's the one who turned the sisters over to the baldfaces. He betrayed us."

Delilah Dogwood growled. The sasquatches backed away, expecting a hairy fit, but her brother raised his well-groomed hand. The crowd stopped moving.

"A strong accusation. It would mean more if it came from a sasquatch," he said.

"I am a sasquatch."

"I meant a real sasquatch. Which you are not. That is as plain as the hairless nose on your hairless face."

The sasquatches shuffled away from me.

"I'm not a baldface," I said, glancing at the rosy sky.

Yolanda Yeti shook her head. "I've known Barnabas since he was knee high to a bear cub. He is no baldface."

Dogger Dogwood pointed down at my tiny feet. "Then how do you explain those?"

A collective gasp rose from the sasquatches as they gaped at my tiny feet.

"The baldfaces have sent one of their own to watch us, to find our weaknesses, and then to capture us," he said. "Who knows how long they have been watching us? All the Bigfoot clan must be baldfaces in disguise."

"Tell them the truth," I pleaded to the Hairysons.

Hannah opened her mouth, but her sister smacked her. She fell silent. Delilah Dogwood grabbed the scruff of my neck and hauled me to my feet. My arms were tied behind my back, so I couldn't resist. The sasquatches shuffled for a closer look at my feet. There were mutters of "baldface" and "traitor."

"I'm not a baldface," I said. "The Bigfoots have protected the tribe for many winters."

The other sasquatches nodded, furrowing their eyebrows at Delilah Dogwood.

"Put him down," Yolanda Yeti ordered. "He's right. If the Bigfoots were baldfaces, why would they protect us for so long?"

The crowd murmured agreement and nodded.

Dogger Dogwood wedged himself between us. "Take the hair out of your eyes, Yolanda Yeti. The Bigfoots are baldface spies. They spent all the moons here earning our trust, but they've been passing information about us to the baldfaces. Waiting for the chance to catch us all. Do you think it's an accident that none of the Bigfoot clan is here right now?"

I struggled against Delilah Dogwood's firm grip. "Lies. You tied us up so the baldfaces could get us, but we got away. Hannah, tell them."

"Aha! He's turned the Hairysons against the tribe," Dogger Dogwood accused. "That's why he keeps asking for their help. This one came into camp reeking of whatever the baldfaces eat. The other one wears baldface hides."

Hannah defended her sister. "We needed to set her broken arm."

"They've become baldface lovers," Delilah Dogwood said, spitting.

Her brother nodded. "Yes. They want to live like them. That's why they betrayed our camp to the baldfaces."

"You just want to smear my name so you can take over as tribe leader," I argued. "You can't prove anything."

"Actually, it's funny you should bring that up. Sister, would you be so kind as to show everyone what you found Barnabas carrying?"

"Gladly, brother." She pushed me toward Dogger Dogwood, who grabbed on to my arms and held me fast. The crowd parted and watched as she walked to a fallen log. She reached behind it and pulled out the rifle I had been using to brace myself. Gasps filled the air as everyone stepped away from me. My chances of winning over the tribe were about as dim as the fading light of sunset.

"We all know what the baldfaces use the boom stick for, don't we?" Dogger Dogwood shouted.

"Sour berries! Barnabas wasn't hunting us!" Hannah shouted.

"Stuff a hairball in it," Dogger Dogwood ordered.

Many hairy hands grabbed Hannah and her sister. They struggled against the sasquatches, pushing them away, but they were soon overpowered. Yolanda Yeti glared at me. "Traitor."

"I can explain," I said. "It's not the hairy tangle he's making it look like."

"Enough," Dogger Dogwood barked. "He's trying to distract us. Slow us down so they can catch up. Well, we're not going to let that happen. We travel tonight."

"You can't," I said. "The Bone Eater! We have to find a safe cave to hide in."

"See! Another ploy to get us to stay put. We travel tonight."

"What about them, brother?" Delilah Dogwood asked, nodding to the Hairysons.

He preened his hair for a few breaths, then cracked a smile. "Well we can't have them running around like loose hair or else they'll lead the baldfaces right to us. Take them to the new cave."

"But that was going to be our new home," Yolanda Yeti argued.

He shook his head. "Not any more. We can't stay here if the baldfaces know where we are. Don't worry. We'll find new caves."

"The traitors will slip out of the cave as soon as we leave them," Lorcan Longfoot said, plucking his frizzy arm hair.

Dogger Dogwood cracked a yellow smile at me as he preened himself. "They won't be going anywhere. I'm going to make sure of that."

Chapter Six

The jagged rock teeth of the cave looked like the jaws of an angry bear about to clamp down on us. If this cave was going to be a sasquatch home, we would have knocked out the overhead rock teeth, but this was not going to be home; it was going to be our prison.

Delilah Dogwood shoved Ruth into the cave first. Then she grabbed Hannah and tossed her in like a cougar tossing her cub into a den. Dogger Dogwood untied the vine around my wrists while the tribe combed the rocky area for large rocks. Yolanda Yeti stood apart from the rock hunters.

She folded her arms across her chest and glared at me. "I trusted your family with my hairy hide. You are the scum on a stagnant pond."

"Yolanda Yeti, my parents didn't want the sasquatchlings to make fun of my tiny feet. That's why they hid them. We're not baldface spies."

"He's lying," Dogger Dogwood said.

"You're the one with the forked tongue," I shot back.

He twisted his grip on my arm, but kept his dingy yellow smile as he looked from me to Yolanda Yeti. "His feet don't lie, and his family's absence is a bald patch that can't be easily covered."

Yolanda Yeti eyed me up and down. "I feel like a fool for thinking they were on our side."

"We all fell for their trick. But not any more." He patted my stubbly cheek a few times, finishing with a hard slap.

"Listen to me, Yolanda Yeti. The Bone Eater is loose in the forest. Protect yourselves," I said. "She will come tonight when the moon is full."

"We're wise to your tricks," Dogger Dogwood said. "Aren't we?"

Yolanda Yeti nodded. Then she shoved me into the cave and walked away.

Dogger Dogwood ordered the others: "Block off the entrance. Then we'll set off. The moon is full, so we'll have enough light to travel by."

"No!" Hannah yelled.

Ruth moved forward. "You are dooming everyone if you travel at night."

I pleaded with the tribe members. "Please, I'm trying to save everyone from the monster of the mountain. You're not safe travelling at night. Find a place to hide. The Bone Eater is coming."

No one listened. Lorcan Longfoot rolled a large boulder to the cave entrance. Other sasquatches added large rocks to the pile, while some of the younger ones placed stones on top, walling us off. Dogger Dogwood didn't lift a finger to help, stroking his black neck hair instead. The hairy truth was that he was sticking us in the safest place on the mountain, while he put the rest of the tribe in hairy danger. I tried one last time to warn the tribe members, but each one of them glared at me with narrow-eyed disgust before they placed their stones in the entrance. Within a few breaths, the wall was already as high as my waist.

Dogger Dogwood urged the tribe, "Hurry up. We have no idea how far away the baldfaces are."

The mention of baldfaces spurred the jumpy Lorcan Longfoot to speed up. He shouted at the others, "They're going to rip our hair from our bodies and turn our skin into baldface hides."

The work sped up and before I knew it the wall was as high as my head. I joined the sisters as we watched our fate sealed with the final rocks clacking into place. I pressed my ear against the pile and listened.

Dogger Dogwood's muffled voiced ordered, "Now let's get going."

"What about your sons?" Yolanda Yeti asked.

"Sister, go back to our camp and leave a marker for Darwin and Deacon. They're bright. They'll figure it out and find us."

I knew Darwin was smart, but I wouldn't use "bright" to describe his brother. On either side of me, Ruth and Hannah tried to pull the rocks away, but they could only free some of the smaller ones wedged between the giant boulders. We were stuck. I turned around and slid to the rocky floor. The sisters gave up after a few breaths and joined me on the ground.

"Great mossy rock, this hairy tangle is your fault," Ruth said.

"What did I do?" I asked.

"You ripped out your hair and you hid your tiny feet."

"You're one to talk," I said. "You swallowed a hairball when I needed your help the most."

"Don't lose your beard over this," Hannah said, trying to step between us.

Ruth shoved her aside. "The Bone Eater is out there. Our parents are out there. And if the monster of the mountains hurts Mom and Dad, I'm blaming Barnabas."

"Blame yourself for not helping me. Why didn't you tell everyone the truth?"

"Go cut off the rest of your hair," she said, snarling.

"Enough!" Hannah shouted. "We didn't say anything because Dogger Dogwood said he'd hurt our parents."

My mouth dropped open. "Ruth, is this true? She turned her back on me.

Her sister explained, "He said he'd turn them over to the baldfaces just like he tried to do with us. I'm sorry, Barnabas."

"It wouldn't have helped even if we did speak up earlier," Ruth mumbled. "Not when the tribe saw the boom stick. Why did you have to take that thing?"

"We needed protection against the Bone Eater," I said.

"A branch would have been just as good."

"I'm sorry, but you didn't complain when Hannah fed you the bag of delicious dirt."

"Eating their food isn't as bad as using one of their weapons," she shot back.

I fumed in silence with my back against the pile of rocks. Ruth stomped away and sat down far from me. Hannah kept plucking rocks away, looking for a way out. After a few breaths, however, she gave up and sat down beside me. In the darkness, my other senses became sharper. I could hear the whistle of air through Ruth's nose. I could smell Hannah's sweaty fear. I could feel the cold rock against my back. The hard stones were like a knot of thigh hair: too thick to untangle. We were trapped.

I calmed myself, imagining the dark cave as the night sky. I saw myself sitting on my favourite ledge with Dad, playing star shapes.

That had been long before any baldfaces showed up on the mountain, before the hunters grabbed me, before Dad had fallen off the cliff. The two of us were just enjoying the night air and making shapes out of stars. I missed him so much. I could feel something wet rolling down my stubbly face, but I wiped the tear away.

I tried to remember the star shape game with Dad. If I squinted hard enough, I could almost make out the light from one of the stars. A faint blue glow. Hairy armpits, this wasn't my imagination. A faint blue glow came from the back of the cave. It wasn't strong, but it was definitely light.

"Do you see what I see?" I asked.

Hannah gasped. "Light."

"Where?" Ruth asked. "Oh!"

"Come on," I said, scrambling to my feet and heading to the light.

"It's not light from a fire," Hannah said. "What if it's light from a baldface machine?"

"If the tribe was going to make this cave our home, they would have searched it and found the baldfaces," Ruth said.

"Wouldn't they have also seen the light?" Hannah asked.

I shook my head. "Not if they arrived here during the day. The light's dim enough that you wouldn't notice it against the sunlight."

"So what's causing it?" Hannah asked.

"Only one way to find out."

Moving in the cramped cave was easier for me, because I could brace myself against a rock tooth or a cave wall. Sometimes I could move several strides without having to steady myself. I had always worn the fake foot hides and relied on them to give me the balance to stay upright, and I began to wonder if they had kept me from learning how to walk on my own.

"Grab a rock, Barnabas," Ruth said. "We need a weapon in case we come across bald-faces."

I kicked around the cave until my toes banged into something hard. I picked up a rock that fit well in the palm of my hand. Hannah grunted as she found rocks for Ruth and herself. We stepped toward the light. As we got closer, I noticed the light was coming from a straight crack, but it wasn't just a crack; it was a section of rock that hid a passageway. I stepped around the wall and the blue glow lit the way. I walked toward the source.

"It's not making any sound. That's good, right?" Ruth whispered.

I shook my head.

"Do you smell that?" Hannah asked, sniffing the dank cave air.

I sniffed. "Bat poo . . . some lingering scent of sasquatch. Must be from the tribe."

"Take another whiff," she ordered.

I did. The musky scent of Hannah and Ruth filled my nostrils, but then I picked up the very faint odour of wolf. Was this the Bone Eater's den?

CHAPTER SEVEN

The thought of being trapped in the Bone Eater's lair made my body hair bristle. I shuddered, remembering the night on a baldface boat when Hannah and I had barely survived against the werewolf Lysander. If Ruth was right about the size of the Bone Eater, we wouldn't have a chance against her. The only thing that gave me hope was the passageway was too low and narrow for a large creature.

I tried to calm the sisters. "No need to worry. The Bone Eater scent is faint, which means even if this is her lair she's out of the cave."

Hannah pulled her rat-tail from behind her head and began to chew on it.

Ruth plucked at her thigh hair. "If the Bone Eater is out there, then no one in the tribe is safe."

"Mom and Dad are out there," her sister added. "And if the Dogwood brothers caught them, they'll be tied up. Which means they'll be helpless."

"Groom your hair," I said. "We don't know where the Bone Eater is right now and your parents are pretty clever. I don't think Darwin and Deacon would have caught them that easily."

"Still, we have to find a way out," Ruth said.

"Maybe the glow will lead us to another exit," I suggested. I moved to the end of the passageway, where I was able to find the source of the light. Sitting on a small rock ledge was a smooth orb about the size of an acorn. The glow seemed to come from the orb's surface. I touched it, expecting to feel warmth, but the orb was as cold as ice. The sisters gathered around the ledge.

"Must be something the baldfaces made."

Hannah disagreed with her sister. "Doesn't smell like rotting lilacs and there are no markings. Baldfaces like to put symbols on all their possessions."

"But if they didn't make the orb, who did?" I asked.

No one had an answer. I picked up the object. "At least this will help us find the way out. Let's go."

Holding the blue orb in front of me, I turned to the left and followed the passageway. The path turned right, then left, then right, then right again. All the while, it felt like we were moving down. I hoped the passageway would lead to an opening further down the mountain, which would put us closer to the valley, and hopefully closer to Ruth and Hannah's parents.

At times the passageway opened up wide enough for the three of us to walk shoulder to shoulder. Other times we had to travel in a single line. Then we came to a fork and had to decide whether or not to go straight, go right, or go left. I decided to go straight, but as I walked about five strides, the orb's light died, leaving us in darkness.

"Ow," Ruth said behind me.

"Are you all right?" Hannah asked.

"The sling is caught on the rock."

"Hold on," I said. "We'll help." I groped the wall, feeling my way back along the passageway. Strangely, the orb began to glow again. Hannah used the light to see while she freed the sling from the jutting rock.

"Okay, follow me," I said. Again, I headed straight, but within three strides the light dimmed again.

"I guess it only works for so long," Hannah said.

"Let me try something. Move back." We stepped backwards and the orb came back to life. "Hairy armpits. I think the orb knows which way to go."

"You mean it's alive?"

"I don't know, but let's see what happens when we go a different way," I said.

I slipped past the sisters and turned down a new passageway. Within three strides, the light faded. When I retraced my steps, it came back to life. I headed into the final passageway, and the orb still glowed even after my tenth stride.

"Come on," I said, waving for the sisters to catch up.

The orb never steered us wrong whenever we came to a fork. Faced with moving in darkness or light, I always chose light. The air grew warmer and heavier as we walked. Then, without warning, the passageway ended in a cavern so large that even with the light I couldn't see the other end. What I did see was a gathering of stone benches around what looked like a pile of orbs like the one I carried. I picked up the scent of hazelnuts and blueberries and my stomach rumbled.

Hannah sniffed the air and turned to her sister.

Ruth smiled. "I smell it too. There's food here."

Hannah combed the area and found a basket behind a bench. It held dark flat squares that smelled of nuts and berries. Ruth and I squatted around the basket. I picked one up and bit into it. While the square was dry, the taste of sweet berries and salty hazelnuts exploded in my mouth and sparked my hunger. I swallowed the treat and picked up another. The sisters also ate from the basket.

"How did these squares get here?" Hannah asked, her question muffled by the food in her mouth.

I shrugged as I ate another square.

Hannah suggested, "Maybe these are the Bone Eater's winter stores."

Ruth shook her head. "You two aren't still trying to convince me the Bone Eater is a sasquatch, are you?" Her mouth was stained purple from the flat treats.

"Hairy armpits, Ruth. Why do you find it so hard to believe this?" I asked.

"I believe the Bone Eater is a monster. You heard the stories about how it eats the bones of sasquatches. Do you think a sasquatch could do this to one of their own?"

"When she turns into the Bone Eater, she forgets she's a sasquatch and becomes this unthinking monster that only wants to feed," I explained. "Trust me, Ruth. I've seen it happen."

"Well, I haven't and I'm not sure you have, either."

We said nothing more, instead choosing to eat the rest of the squares in silence. When I was done, I held the orb up, trying to see how high the cavern was, but the light wasn't strong enough.

"Let me see the orb, Barnabas," Hannah said, sitting on a stone bench near the edge of the pile.

I tossed the glowing object to her. As it sailed over the pile of orbs, they lit up. Ruth gasped. Hannah nearly dropped the falling orb.

"Sour berries," Hannah gasped. "What are these things?"

We gathered around the pile, but the glow began to fade.

"Hannah, drop the orb on them," I ordered.

When she did, the other orbs began to glow brighter. We stepped back and watched as the glow from the pile grew brighter and stronger until the entire cavern lit up as light bounced off the overhead crystal rock teeth. The cavern was large, maybe three or four hundred strides long and two hundred strides wide. The rocky floor looked like black ice but felt warm. Across the shiny surface was a design that appeared to be a blue snowflake with lines running out from the centre and spreading out like a spider web, with crescent moon markings every few strides. One of the lines led to the far end of the cavern, where I thought I saw the thin outline of a glowing door set against the rock.

"Great mossy rock, what is this place?" Ruth asked.

"I don't have a hairy idea," her sister said.

I took a guess. "There are four benches around the pile, which means it's a place for many. It could be a den, but I don't see any bedrocks, so I don't think you're meant to stay here for very long. The basket of nut and berry squares doesn't hold enough to last the winter, just enough for a few meals. Maybe this is a place to rest on a long journey."

"Journey to where?" Hannah asked.

"And who's doing the travelling?" Ruth added.

A tangled knot began to form in my mind. Why was there more than one stone bench? If this was the Bone Eater's lair, why did she need so many places to sit? What if there was more than one of her? I didn't like the answers I came up with and I decided to keep them to myself. Instead, I picked up the orb from the pile. The pile of orbs dimmed. The brilliant roof of crystal rock teeth disappeared from our view and darkness returned.

"Now what do we do?" Ruth asked.

"We follow the orb," Hannah said.

The sisters got up, but I froze. Behind them was a pair of glowing red eyes.

CHAPTER EIGHT

Grandma Bertha had a saying: "If you're not invited to a cave, there's a hairy good chance that you're not welcome."

I'd never understood what she meant until right now. I couldn't feel less welcome with the red eyes glaring at me from the darkness. I stepped back, motioning Hannah and Ruth to get up and follow me. I led the sisters toward the entrance at the other end of the cavern. We took about four steps before we heard a low growl. I slowed down, but kept walking.

"There are three of us and only one of it," Hannah said. "We could wrestle it to the ground."

Ruth whispered, "What if it's the Bone Eater?"

The creature smelled like a wolf, but it seemed too small to be the monster that had destroyed the baldface camp. Even if it wasn't the Bone Eater, this creature could still be dangerous. The growling grew louder as we walked and the red-eyed beast began to advance, its paws thudding on the rock floor.

"Run!" I yelled as I ran toward the entrance at the far end of the cavern, using the glowing orb to light our escape. We slipped into a passageway and entered a maze. I turned right and sprinted. Then I reached a fork in the passageway and slipped to the left. I couldn't hear the creature behind us, but I wasn't about to stop and check.

I rounded a corner and chose a passageway to the left and sprinted as fast as I could. As I ran, the orb light began to fade. I had chosen the wrong path, but there was no way I could double back. The sisters were shoving me forward. I ran ahead, willing the orb to stay lit. A dozen strides later, we were plunged into darkness. I ran three strides and smacked nose first into a rock wall. Putting out my hands, I felt along the smooth rock surface, moving to the left. I dropped the orb, reached back with one hand and touched Hannah's leg.

"This way," I said. "Make sure Ruth is with us too."

"I can't see," Hannah said.

"Follow the sound of my voice," I said, moving along the rock surface.

My voice echoed off the walls and then faded away. All I could hear was the steady padding of paws on rock moving in our direction.

"Forget my voice," I whispered. "Reach out and touch me, Hannah." Her hairy hand groped my back.

"I feel you, Barnabas," she said.

"Then reach back and grab Ruth. We'll stay together like this."

"Okay, Barnabas, I have her."

"Hurry," Ruth hissed. "It's getting closer."

The dark wrapped around me like heavy brush, invisible thorns pricking my body and uneven roots tripping my feet. The air was thick and almost seemed to push me back. Even though my hands were pressed against the rock wall and I could feel the ground under each step, I couldn't shake the hairy feeling that I was going to fall. To put my mind at ease,

I reached out for the other wall. It was there. I dragged my hands along either wall, with Hannah clutching strands of my back hair, and hoped she had a good grip on her sister's hand. The padding footsteps picked up the pace.

I stretched out my strides and felt a sharp tug on my hair until Ruth matched my pace. I wanted to run, but I knew if I went too quickly I might lose Hannah and Ruth. I groped my way along the walls, counting my breaths as I walked. I soon lost track. The dark had a way of stretching out time.

Suddenly, my hands lost contact with both walls. I froze. The Hairysons bashed into my back, sending me forward. I put my hands out to steady myself and found a wall ahead of me. I guessed that we had reached another fork. I caught my breath and listened for the footsteps. Nothing.

"We lost it," Ruth whispered.

The footsteps started again, moving fast. The creature had sharp hearing.

"You're too slow, Barnabas. I'm taking the lead." Hannah moved around me. "Grab on."

I obeyed, reaching back and feeling around until I grabbed Ruth's arm.

"Ow. That's my broken one." She clamped her good hand around my wrist.

If the feeling of walking in the dark with my hands on the walls was unsettling, walking in the dark with no walls to ground or guide me was hair-ible. I felt like the ground would give away at any breath and plunge me into a deep chasm. As we trotted ahead, I couldn't help but think of my dad and how he had fallen off the mountain. I held out hope that he had saved himself.

I imagined he was still alive and that we were picking vegetables from our garden and brushing off the dirt. I could almost hear his deep voice as he warned me not to let the carrots get to my head. Then he tossed carrots at me, starting a food fight. We tossed vegetables at each other, laughing, until Mom came out and scolded us. He grabbed my hand and bolted away from her as she chased us through the woods. I could almost see his open-mouthed laugh as he turned to taunt Mom. I could almost smell the musky scent from his hairy chest. I felt the cool breeze of the mountain air rush past us as we ran. Hairy armpits! The air was real.

"Hannah, do you feel that?"

She kept walking. "We can't stop now." Ruth said, "I feel it too. It's fresh air. Where's it coming from?"

"I don't know." I sniffed the air. Pine and fir. We were near an entrance, but Hannah refused to stop or slow down. The footsteps behind us spurred her faster. Was this creature the Bone Eater or was it something that the Bone Eater had bitten and turned into another monster? How many monsters might be running around inside the mountain? These questions became a hairy tangle in my mind as I ran after Hannah. Grandma Bertha had a saying: "Know your enemy as well as you know yourself." If we were going to defeat the Bone Eater, we had to know all about it.

Suddenly, Hannah screamed and fell forward. I let go of Ruth and grabbed Hannah's back hair, trying to get a good grip around her waist. She teetered in front of me. I skidded along the ground, fighting to keep her upright. Ruth grabbed me with her good arm and steadied the two of us.

We pulled Hannah back, but as we did I saw her faint outline against a blue glow below. She had almost stepped off a cliff into a chasm. Below, there was an eerie blue light. I peeked over the edge, looking for the source. I couldn't see anything except the faint glow far below us.

The creature growled about fifty strides behind us. I scanned the ledge for a way down, but found nothing.

"This way," Ruth said, pulling me to the right, where there was a narrow lip of rock.

We stepped along the ledge over the chasm and the blue glow. I wished I had the baldface rifle with me so I could get a closer look at what was down there. The ledge began to narrow and I had to turn my attention to where I was going, grabbing the rocky outcroppings to steady myself as we moved up. The fresh scent of pine filled my nostrils. Ruth had found the way out. A low growl behind us, but the creature didn't follow. I looked back, hoping to catch a glimpse, but I only spotted a hulking figure against the glow.

Finally we reached the surface, coming out of a narrow opening at the base of an old tree that had seen better days. The twisted tree had a wide trunk and gnarly roots, but it had been many winters since the branches bore any leaves. I had to push Ruth's butt to get her through the opening and she howled when her broken arm scraped against the side of the hole. I followed, receiving the same butt push from Hannah. Then I turned and pulled her through.

The moon cast a pale light on the valley before us. We had come back to where I first saw Yolanda Yeti. The breeze felt good against my bare face. I closed my eyes and listened to a hawk owl hooting in the distance. It was drowned out by a roar which didn't sound like rapids or a waterfall. I opened my eyes and spotted beams of lights sweeping across the woods below. The roar came from a machine. Hairy armpits! The baldfaces were here.

Chapter Nine

Hannah stiffened. Ruth let out a low growl as the lights from the baldfaces moved across the valley. They were definitely on the hunt. Hannah chewed on her rat-tail while her sister twisted her moustache nervously.

"Do you think they've found the tribe?" Hannah asked.

I shook my head. "Not unless Dogger Dogwood led the tribe back this way. If he's smart, he's headed higher up the mountain."

Ruth pointed at the lights. "The baldfaces are looking for something. Why else travel at night?"

"Maybe it's the Bone Eater," I suggested.

She shook her head. "If it was the Bone Eater, they'd be running in the opposite direction."

My stomach lurched with the truth. "When I was watching you two in the camp, the Dogwood brothers walked past me. I overheard them talking. They were supposed to look for your parents."

Hannah stiffened. "He told us to keep quiet or else he'd give up Mom and Dad to the bald-faces."

Ruth slapped her hand on her thigh. "Our parents might be in the valley. We have to find them before the baldfaces do."

"They might have escaped on their own," I said.

"Sour berries! We can't take the chance," Hannah said. "We're wasting breath standing here. We have to find them." She sprinted down the slope, waving for us to follow.

"Wait!" I said. "We don't know what traps they might have set. You can't just charge at them."

She was beyond listening to reason. I sighed and gave chase, trying to keep up. Ruth joined me. The uneven surface was hard on my feet, and I realized that in the cavern I didn't feel any pain in my soles because the ground was flat and smooth. Out here, the ground was rough and unforgiving.

Hannah slowed down as she neared the beams of light, giving Ruth and me a chance to catch up. We huddled behind heavy brush, bracketed by two tall spruce trees. We watched a baldface hunter walk through the woods, sweeping his light across. The beam danced around our location, and we ducked until he moved on.

Hannah pointed to her nose. I sniffed the air. The odour of rotting lilacs punched up my nose. I tried to ignore the baldface smell, taking a deeper whiff until I picked up the scent of sasquatch.

Ruth grabbed her sister. "I smell them. Can you?"

Hannah smiled. "Yes. Wait." She sniffed again. "There's someone else."

I lifted my nose to the air and sucked in the scents wafting in the wind. "I know that smell. It's Dogwood."

She looked at me, her furry eyebrows knitting together with concern. "Which one?"

I shrugged. I had no idea.

Ruth smacked my arm. "Forget the Dogwoods. We have to get closer to the bald-faces and see what's going on."

Hannah agreed. "I can smell Dad's fear. They're in trouble."

I shook my head. "We have to be careful. I don't want to end up in another cage."

She glared at me. "You can stay here if you're too scared, Barnabas."

"Groom your hair. Yes, I'm scared. Scared is smart, because being scared means you'll be careful and won't make mistakes. If the bald-faces have your parents, they would have left the valley. Have you thought that maybe the baldfaces are using your parents as bait?"

This silenced her.

"This is a hairy tangle," I said. "And the only way to unravel it is to find out why the bald-faces are still here."

"He's right," Ruth mumbled.

Hannah said nothing.

"Okay, then. Ruth, stay low and keep an eye out for anyone who might try to sneak up on us. Hannah, climb up the tree and scout the area. We'll wait until they move past us, then I'll move behind them and follow. Go."

Hannah was up the tree faster than a squirrel. Her sister lowered herself behind the brush. I scanned the valley floor. While I couldn't see any more baldfaces, I could hear them moving through the brush. I closed my eyes and counted my breaths. By the time I reached thirty, Hannah was back on the ground.

"They're past us, Barnabas."

I patted Ruth on the back. "Whistle three times if you see a baldface, then take Hannah to high ground. No matter what happens, don't try to follow me. Understand?"

She nodded. I headed after the baldfaces. I soon reached the edge of the group of hunters. A shivering baldface with a light stick swept his beam across the woods and lit up the face of an approaching baldface, who shielded his eyes.

"Lower the flashlight, dude," the stocky hunter ordered as he moved closer.

"Any sign of the sasquatch?" the cold baldface asked.

"Naw. But we should call it quits while we're ahead. You know that saying. One in the hand is worth two in the bush."

"Okay, I'll tell Perkins you want to quit," the shivering baldface said.

"No way. That guy scares me. Wouldn't surprise me if he had a few screws loose."

"Watch your mouth. The guy can sneak up on you any time. He's a ninja."

"Yeah, it's creepy how he does that," the stocky hunter said, glancing behind himself.

The shivering baldface blew into his hands. "Oh man, I can't even feel my fingers, it's so cold."

"Thought you might be freezing. Here, I brought you some coffee. Give me some light."

The baldface aimed his light at his companion, who held a silver container with a black top. He unscrewed the black top and the smell of delicious dirt filled the night air.

The shivering baldface took the black top and drank from it. "Thanks. I needed that. So what are you going to do with your share of Roland's reward?"

"I'm going to buy me a brand new pick-up. Hemi engine. Wide box. The works. You?"

"I'm going to get a flat-screen TV. Get rid of my crappy forty-inch plasma and get me a seventy-inch LCD screen."

"Sweet," the stocky hunter said. "I can't wait to cash in."

Nothing ever seemed to be enough for baldfaces. That much I'd learned from my brief time among them. They used something called money to buy what they wanted. And they never seemed to have enough money to get what they wanted, or when they got what they wanted they wanted something else. Often, when baldfaces camped at the base of my old mountain home, they'd leave many of their things behind. One time Dad found plates that we used for our meals. Another time, they left the foot hides that I had used to disguise my small feet. It seemed that once baldfaces got what they wanted, they took it for granted, which was why it was so easy for them to throw away their things. I wondered if they would throw out the Hairysons once they were done with them.

"Okay, you keep a sharp eye out. The sooner we get that last sasquatch, the quicker we can get back to camp," the stocky hunter said, taking the top back and screwing it on the silver container.

The shivering baldface headed away. I decided to follow the stocky hunter, staying low in the brush. I slunk behind him as he led me to a makeshift camp where four hunters were gathered around a fire. They jumped up and lifted their rifles when the stocky hunter came within the light, but lowered them when they recognized their friend.

"Any sign?" a tall, lanky baldface asked.

"No, Perkins. Nothing."

"We're not leaving this valley until we bag it." Perkins lowered himself onto a blue bench with a high back.

The stocky hunter sat with the others around the fire. The smell of smoke filled the night air and sparks jumped from the fire, popping as wood knots exploded. I moved closer to the hunters, then I picked up the smell of sasquatch. I moved toward the smell and found the Hairysons. Juniper and Hemlock Hairyson were seated on the ground, bound to each other, back to back. Their arms were tied together and so were their feet. Their heads were bowed and I could hear heavy snoring, but it wasn't coming from them. The noise was coming from a sasquatch sleeping on the other side of them. Darwin Dogwood.

"Psst," I whispered. "Don't have a hairy fit. It's me. Barnabas Bigfoot."

"Barnabas?" Hemlock Hairyson whispered back. "What are you doing here?"

"I'm here to save you," I said.

"Lopsided linden tree, you shouldn't have come here," Juniper Hairyson said.

I glanced back at the hunters, but they paid no attention to us. They were all talking about what they would do with their sasquatch reward. I moved closer to the Hairysons, but I was careful to stay in the dark, so they wouldn't see my bare face. I recalled the looks of horror when the tribe members saw me.

"Are Hannah and Ruth with you?" she asked. "Are they safe?"

"Yes. We're here to rescue you."

"I won't have you risk my daughters' safety. Is that understood?"

"I doubt the children are going to sit back and do nothing," Hemlock Hairyson said.

"They will if Barnabas tells them that I'll twist their neck hairs into a knot if they even think about risking their hides."

Darwin Dogwood grumbled and rolled over. I glanced back at the hunters. They were deep in their discussion about things they wanted to buy.

"Who are the baldfaces looking for?" I asked.

"Deacon," Juniper Hairyson answered. "But they won't get him. He hightailed it out of here as soon as the baldfaces shot this one."

Darwin snored.

"He seems all right," Hemlock Hairyson said.

"He deserves worse for what he and his brother did," she said, snarling. "They tried to turn us over to the — "

"We can talk about that later," I said. "Right now, I have to get you out. I'm going to untie you and then we'll slip out of the baldface camp."

I crawled over to untie Juniper Hairyson's arms. She let out a gasp as she saw my face. The light from the fire was bright enough to light up both our faces. "What happened to your face? Did the baldfaces do that to you?"

"It's a long story, but trust me, I'm okay. Hold on, this knot is tight. I'm going to have to bite through it."

"Well, well, well, what do we have here?" Perkins' voice called out.

I swung around. Backlit by the orange glow from the campfire, four baldfaces stood a few strides away, their rifles raised at me.

CHAPTER TEN

Hairy armpits! How had the baldfaces snuck up on me? Juniper and Hemlock Hairyson were still tied up, so they were going to be no help, and Darwin was still snoring. I stood up and turned around. The baldfaces aimed their rifles at me.

"Hold up," Perkins said. He pulled a thick stick from inside his hide and turned it on, pointing the light at me. I shielded my eyes from the glare. "Easy, boys. Looks like we got ourselves a joker. What in the blue blazes do you think you're doing out here in that costume?"

He thought I was a baldface. The other hunters lowered their weapons. I breathed a sigh of relief, glad for my bare face.

"Kid, you could have been hurt. What were you thinking?" Perkins asked.

I said nothing.

"Who are you with anyway? Oh man, you're not PETA, are you? I'm sick of those jerks running around the woods and getting in our way. You with them?"

If I didn't answer his questions soon, he might start to see through my disguise. I moved away from the Hairysons and tried my best to be a baldface, recalling the ones I had seen in the mall when I was first captured. I crossed my arms over my chest, dropped one shoulder and spit on the ground. "Yeah. So?"

"You here on your own?"

I shrugged.

"Oh man, don't tell me you got pals in the trees with video cameras."

"Maybe." I had no idea what he was saying, but the less I said, the better my chances of coming across as one of them.

"Don't play smart with me, kid. Where are your organic wheat-bread-eating pals?"

The baldfaces seemed to have a few hairs out of place, and I wasn't about to help them groom themselves.

"They're around," I said. "They've seen everything. You're in a hairy tangle."

"A what?"

"Trouble," I said. "Lots of trouble."

Perkins laughed. The other baldfaces snickered. "From a college kid running around in a gorilla suit?"

They weren't taking the bait. I had to try something else. "You think you've captured sasquatches, but you haven't. They're like me."

Perkins rubbed his chin and walked close enough that I could see his icy blue eyes. He ran his hand across the stubble on the top of his head and sighed. "You really think we're that stupid. We checked their hair. It's part of their bodies, not like your gorilla suit."

He reached out to grab my arm.

"Stay back," I said.

"Take that stupid gorilla costume off." He took my wrist and started to pull at the hair. Hairy armpits, he had a strong grip. I winced as he pulled.

"It has to be a suit," Perkins said, pulling at my chest hair and then my leg hair. "It has to be a . . . a . . . what are you?" He began to back away from me. The other baldfaces came closer, confused.

"What's wrong, Perkins?" the stocky hunter asked.

"It's not a suit. It's real hair."

"But, but, but he can talk."

Perkins raised his rifle at me. "What are you?"

I said nothing more. The others raised their rifles.

Suddenly, a rock struck Perkins on the side of the head. He staggered forward, reeling. The next few breaths were a hairy tangle as the dark woods erupted. Rocks pelted the bald-faces, forcing them back. Two of the baldfaces ran to the other side of the fire, trying to get away from the rocks. The stocky hunter knelt and aimed his rifle at the source of the flying rocks.

"No!" I yelled.

I leapt at the stocky hunter, pushing him off balance as he tried to fire. One of the retreating baldfaces yelped in pain.

"You shot me!" he yelled. "You shot . . . meeee." He yawned as he flopped to the ground.

Perkins pulled out a black box and yelled into it: "Help! We're under attack!"

The stocky hunter swung his rifle at the woods and fired. No one was paying attention to me. I rushed to the Hairysons, wedged myself between them, and bit into the bonds that held Juniper Hairyson's arms. "Can you untie your feet?" I asked.

"Yes. Help Hemlock."

I leaned down and bit through his bonds. He pulled his arms free and started to untie his legs. Meanwhile Darwin sat up, his eyes wide and his ear hair up on end. I rushed over and freed his hands. Another volley of rocks drove the baldfaces back, but they returned fire, their rifles hiccupping as they sent sleeping arrows into the darkness.

Juniper Hairyson stood and helped her mate to his feet. "Barnabas, run! Before they hit my daughters."

She sprinted away, pulling Hemlock Hairyson with her. A fresh round of rocks pelted the three baldfaces, driving them back. One rock struck the stocky hunter in the face. He dropped his weapon and clutched his nose in pain. The sisters had incredible aim.

The Hairysons were several strides away. I started to follow, but Darwin grabbed me, his legs still tied together. "Don't leave me. Please."

"Come on," Juniper Hairyson called.

Grandma Bertha had a saying about the importance of the tribe: "A tree alone will always fall, but a forest stands forever." As rotten as the Dogwood family was, I couldn't abandon him. Grandma Bertha wouldn't leave him behind. My mother wouldn't leave him behind. I couldn't leave him behind. I reached out and grabbed his hand, pulling him to his feet. I hooked his arm around my neck and dragged him toward the Hairysons.

Then, just as suddenly as the rocks had flown at the baldfaces, they stopped. Perkins turned around and saw us. He raised his rifle. The others turned their rifles on us as well.

"You're not going anywhere," he said.

The shivering baldface I had seen earlier emerged from the woods, along with a half dozen others. They surrounded Hannah and Ruth, herding them toward us, herding them with their rifles. The sisters said nothing. I shook my head at the Hairysons and put my finger to my lips. They nodded. Darwin moaned. I shushed him.

Perkins shook his head, smiling. "Six sasquatches. What a payday. And if they can all talk like this bald-faced one, I'm asking for more money."

I didn't know what to make of a baldface calling me a baldface. On the one foot, he was right. My face was hairless, but on the other foot, I was nothing like a baldface. I wouldn't tear up creatures' homes or hunt them down. I decided baldface was a hair-ible insult and I bared my teeth at Perkins. All he did was chuckle and rub his hands together.

The stocky hunter, still clutching his bloodied nose, squinted at the sisters. "The sasquatch we were chasing had black hair."

Perkins cracked a huge grin. "Years of searching and we can't even find a footprint, and now . . . Oh man, Mr. Roland is going to make us rich."

The baldfaces clapped each other on the back and slapped each other's raised hands. Then a group of eight more baldfaces roared into camp atop red machines that were belching smoke. One baldface with long sideburns and black hair tied in a rat-tail like Hannah's hopped off and ran to Perkins. He smiled when he saw all of us. "You've been busy, Perkins."

"Any luck tracking the one that got away, Myron?"

Sideburns shook his head. "It went up into the mountains. We lost it."

Perkins sighed. "There's another hour to sunrise. I'll pick up the trail."

The stocky hunter asked, "What do we do about them?"

"We'll split up. I'll take Myron and a couple of other trackers up the mountain. The rest of you will escort our new friends back to camp. It'll be a tight squeeze, but they should all fit in the cage."

This seemed to make the stocky hunter happy. Myron clapped his hand on Perkins' shoulder. The celebration was cut short by the sound of a roar that seemed to shake the entire forest and maybe even the mountains. The overpowering scent of sasquatch and wolf filled my nose. The Bone Eater was here.

CHAPTER ELEVEN

The baldfaces grabbed their rifles as the Bone Eater's roar echoed through the valley. My heart beat hard and fast in my chest as I scanned the area for the monster of the mountains. I couldn't see her but I knew she was near.

"Protect the cargo!" Perkins yelled.

Baldfaces formed a ring around us, pointing their weapons in all directions. Perkins and Myron stamped out the fire. Light sticks came to life and swept the woods.

Another roar shook the valley. The hunters behind me gasped. Giant pine trees crashed to the ground as if they were saplings. There, rising up, filling in the gap between the fallen trees, was the Bone Eater. Ruth hadn't been pulling our hair when she'd said this monster was huge. She was almost as tall as the tree she stood beside. The beams of light swung toward her, revealing matted black hair and a giant head. The Bone Eater bared her long, sharp fangs, which were as thick as logs. What was most striking about the Bone Eater was her fierce eyes, which were as big as twin full moons.

"That's the mother of all sasquatches," Myron shouted.

"Shoot it!" Perkins yelled.

The hiccupping rifles answered his call to action, but the sleeping arrows were like mosquitoes to the Bone Eater. She swatted at them, then scooped up one of the fallen trees and raised it over her head.

"Aim for the eyes!" Myron ordered.

I leaned to Hannah. "I have an idea. Stay close."

She moved behind me. The Bone Eater hurled the tree in our direction. It crashed on the ground, sending branches and bushes flying in the air. The baldfaces screamed as they scattered for cover. Perkins and Myron barked orders at them to stand their ground. The Bone Eater picked up another tree to hurl.

The hunters kept firing. She roared and hurled the tree, which landed a few strides away. Bark chunks pelted me.

The circle around us was now broken up, leaving gaps for us to slip through. We backed away. I knew the monster of the mountains wanted to chew our bones, which meant the sooner we left, the better.

"Hairy armpits," I said. "Let's run!"

Juniper Hairyson grabbed Hannah and bolted away.

Perkins turned and yelled, "The sasquatches are getting away. Stop them!"

No one listened. They were too busy shooting at the Bone Eater.

Hemlock Hairyson reached for Ruth, but a panicked Darwin got between the two in his rush to get away. Ruth stumbled forward a few steps and fell to the ground.

"Don't worry," I said. "I'll get her. Follow Hannah."

I rushed to Ruth's side, but Perkins jumped over her as he pulled out a black stick. It was shorter than the rifle, but the tip of it crackled with blue lightning.

"You're not going anywhere," he said. "Not one step. You know what this is?"

I froze, not moving, not even breathing, my hairs bristling.

"It's an electric prod," he said. "State of the art. It'll put down a rhino."

I stepped back.

"Stay where you are," he ordered. "Or else."

He jabbed the black stick into Ruth's stomach. Blue lightning danced from the stick into her hair. She howled in pain. The Bone Eater roared in answer and started to lumber toward us.

"That's just the low setting," Perkins said. He turned a knob at the bottom of the stick. "This is medium. Now get on your knees. I'm not losing my prize."

"My insides are on fire!" Ruth yelped.

The Bone Eater roared in response. The baldfaces fired their rifles, but the sleeping arrows had no effect.

"Get on your knees!" Perkins yelled, pointing the prod at Ruth's stomach.

"Don't!" I yelled.

"Down. Now," he said, jabbing Ruth again.

She howled in pain, a high-pitched yip that cut through the night. The Bone Eater howled and charged toward us. Each step she took shook the earth as she made a beeline toward Perkins. Brush flew up along with huge clumps of dirt. The baldfaces stayed and fired, but then they broke ranks and ran. Only Perkins and Myron stood their ground.

"Perkins! Turn around," Myron called.

But Perkins was too interested in me. "You don't want me to set this thing to high."

Before I could drop down, the Bone Eater swatted at Perkins, catching both him and Myron with a sweep of her hand, sending the two hunters flying through the air. I backed away as she let out another roar.

"Give me your hand, Ruth!" I screamed.

She sat up and saw the Bone Eater. "Great mossy rock," she said.

Before I could get to her, the beast had scooped her up.

"Put her down!" I yelled.

The Bone Eater bellowed. The force of the air from her foul mouth knocked me to the ground, sending me tumbling end over end like I was a blown leaf in a windstorm. When I came to rest, hairy hands reached down to help me up. Hannah was by my side, along with her parents. Darwin gaped at the scene unfolding before him, muttering to himself: "Impossible. Impossible."

I swept my hair out of my eyes and watched the Bone Eater lumber away.

"Ruth!" Juniper Hairyson screamed as she started forward.

Hemlock Hairyson grabbed her around the waist and held her back.

The Bone Eater let out one final roar at the baldfaces, then turned and strode toward the gap she had created in the tree line. In the blink of an eye, she and Ruth were gone.

Chapter Twelve

"We have to go after them," Juniper Hairyson said, straining to break free from Hannah and Hemlock Hairyson.

"We can't, Mom. Look at the valley. The baldfaces are everywhere."

"Hannah's right," I said. "It won't take long for the hunters to regroup. They'll want to catch us again. The best thing we can do for Ruth is slip away. I promise we'll find Ruth, but we can't do that if we're in a cage."

Darwin muttered, "No way Ruth's alive. The monster's going to eat her."

"Stuff your hair in your mouth," Hannah said.

"Don't listen to him," I pleaded. "I will save Ruth."

"No one can save her," Darwin said, shaking his head and nervously rubbing his black beard.

"My sweet furball," Juniper Hairyson sobbed.

Hemlock Hairyson growled at Darwin. "You're lucky you're even here. If it weren't for Barnabas . . . "

I interrupted. "Groom your hair. Darwin is a part of this tribe and we'll need him if we're going to rescue Ruth."

"She's alone against the beast," Juniper Hairyson said.

Hannah stroked her mom's long brown hair. "She'll be all right. She's tough and smart. She's stronger than anyone in the tribe."

Darwin crossed his arms over his chest. "I'm not going anywhere near the Bone Eater. I like my bones the way they are."

"You need us to keep the baldfaces away," I said.

In that breath, he revealed his true Dogwood colours, cowering at the mention of baldfaces. "They don't care about us any more. They'll want the Bone Eater."

117

I shook my head. "They get a reward for every sasquatch they catch."

Juniper Hairyson backed me up. "Yes, I heard them talking about how sasquatches were valuable. They won't stop until they catch us again."

"You can part your hair any way you want, Darwin," I said. "Will you help us or take your chances with the baldfaces?"

At first he said nothing, glaring from me to the others. Finally he sighed. "What do we need to do?"

"First, we have to get the hunters out of our hair," I said. "Hannah, you ready for a game of baldface chase?"

She nodded. "What were you thinking?"

"Lead them to the cavern opening. Make them think we went inside. If we're lucky, they'll meet the red-eyed creature in the mountain."

She cracked a gap-toothed grin. "Sweet cherries. Good idea."

Darwin said, "You don't need me for that. What do *I* do?"

"You help the Hairysons track the Bone Eater." I turned to Hannah's parents "Follow the trail. I'm pretty sure the last thing the baldfaces want to do is tangle with the Bone Eater again. You'll be safe from the hunters."

Darwin cut in. "I'm not going after the monster."

I glanced at the full moon, which was starting to set. "You'll be all right."

"Bald patch," he said. "You saw what the creature did."

I nodded. "Okay, so that means you're willing to take your chances with the baldfaces. I never thought you'd be so brave."

"Uh, I didn't say that."

Hemlock Hairyson grunted. "Don't worry, I'll protect you, Darwin."

He said nothing, but slunk off to the side, far away from Hannah and me.

Juniper Hairyson clapped her hand on my shoulder. "Nothing's going to stop me from getting my daughter back."

I smiled at her. "The best way to track them is to sniff for Ruth."

Hemlock Hairyson snorted. "I think the Bone Eater left us a pretty good trail to follow."

I wanted to tell them the Bone Eater would change into Daphne Dogwood by the time the sun rose, but I remembered how Ruth had laughed at me when I told her. There was no way the Hairysons would believe the monster of the mountains was actually one of our own. Besides, right now the only thing that mattered to the Hairysons was Ruth.

"Hannah and I will catch up to you as soon as we can."

Juniper Hairyson nodded and led her mate and Darwin toward the Bone Eater's wide trail. She angled her path to avoid the baldface camp. Once they were on their way, Hannah and I trekked through the woods toward the baldfaces, breaking branches and overturning stones. We wanted to leave an easy trail for the baldfaces to follow.

She tore off some hair and hooked it around a branch. "Do you think Ruth will be all right?"

"Look at the sky. The Bone Eater will change soon."

"You saw the monster. She could eat my sister right now."

"The monster is probably taking Ruth to her lair, which can't be close by or else she would have attacked the baldface camp long before we stumbled across it. There's a good chance that by the time she reaches her lair, the moon will set and she'll be Daphne Dogwood again."

"That's what worries me. What will Daphne Dogwood do? If she was abandoned by the tribe, what will she do when she finally sees one of our own?"

I hadn't thought of that. "We'd better hurry. You beat a trail to the cavern opening, I'll get the baldfaces' attention."

She trudged through the woods, leaving a trail clear enough for even a one-eyed, stuffy-nosed coyote to follow. As I watched her go, I could feel my chest hair twisting into knots. I knew how hard it was to lose someone close. When I saw my dad fall, it took both sisters to drag me away. All I'd wanted to do was run to my dad and save him. I was sure Hannah wanted to join her parents and search for Ruth. Grandma Bertha would have called Hannah "strong of hair," which meant she had a good heart and a generous tribe spirit.

Hannah understood that we had to get the baldfaces off our backs; there was no point in rescuing Ruth from the Bone Eater only to fall back into the hunters' clutches. She was no longer the bratty sasquatchling who had teased me about my curly beard just a few sunsets ago. Now she was a full-grown sasquatch who was my best friend. I wasn't about to let her down.

Perkins and Myron rallied the hunters back to the campfire. The beams of light swept across the area as the baldfaces called to each other to gather back at the camp. A few of them trained their beams of light on the gap in the trees where the Bone Eater had left. I crept closer.

Perkins barked orders. "Check the ammunition. Do we have bullets?"

Myron yelled back, "No. Roland insisted that the creatures be taken alive. We have plenty of tranq darts left."

"They did no good against the beast. I don't think any of the tranqs penetrated the hide."

A flurry of questions erupted from the surrounding baldfaces: "What was it? Was it one of the sasquatches? Do you think the beast will come back? Do we go after the monster? Should we get reinforcements?"

Perkins waved for silence. "We don't have enough firepower to go after that creature today. To take down that thing we're going to need elephant rifles. We take what we have left and hunt the sasquatches that got away. I need trackers to fan out and comb the area for their trail."

Myron ordered, "Jarvis. Rick. You're with me."

Perkins held his hand up. "As soon as you pick up the trail, call me. We'll assemble a team to get them. Do not approach on your own. I don't want any more surprises. Do I make myself understood?"

A chorus of "yes sirs" filled the air. Myron led two baldfaces away from the main group while Perkins ordered the remaining hunters around. They collected their things and grabbed sleeping arrows for their rifles. I moved along the edge of the trees, keeping pace with the trio as they headed toward the woods, then I stretched out my strides to beat them to the woods so I could mark a trail for them. Unlike the Baldface Chase game I had played earlier, I couldn't let these hunters see me or else they'd shoot me. Instead I had to leave them signs to follow: a snapped branch; a footprint; a patch of trampled grass.

It didn't take long for Myron to pick up the trail. While I couldn't see him, I did hear him barking orders to the others. The scent of rotting lilacs grew stronger. I didn't know if I'd lured all of them to the trail, but there were certainly a lot of baldfaces coming into the woods. I marked my trail, finding my way back to the edge of the clearing. Only four baldfaces remained. Good enough. I headed through the woods to find Hannah.

She waited for me by the rotted tree near the opening. She chewed her rat-tail nervously and spat it out when she spotted me. She motioned for me to back up. I took three steps back and she motioned for me to stop, then pointed to the fir tree to my right. She pointed up. I started to climb. When I reached the lower branches, I worked my way across to a nearby tree and then jumped to the next. When I was far enough away from the trail, I climbed down and joined Hannah.

"Good work," I said. "Now let's put a few strides between us and the trail in case the baldfaces catch on."

We headed through the woods, careful not to make any noise. Soon we heard the voices of many baldfaces. They had taken the bait. I squatted low, waving to her to do the same.

We waited. The scent of baldfaces began to fade away. They were further up the trail. She started to stand, but I pulled her down.

A few breaths later I heard the faraway sound of excited shouts. The baldfaces had found the opening. The cavern would keep them busy long enough for us to get away. We moved through the woods back to the trail that she had left and doubled back to the valley. I stopped at the edge of the tree line and watched the four baldfaces guarding ten red machines. Among them was Perkins, his tall lanky form towering above the others. The rising sun cast a pale glow over the clearing, lighting the faces of the baldfaces. They looked scared, constantly peeking at the gap in the trees where the Bone Eater had appeared.

Perkins spoke into a little black box in his hand. "Myron, I don't care what the men say they hear. Get them in the hole and bring me back my sasquatches."

I nodded to Hannah and we moved around the clearing, sticking to the woods. When we reached the Bone Eater's trail, the valley was bathed in the morning light. We sprinted up the trail that led toward one of the mountains. The monster of the mountains had left a path of destruction. She pushed over trees and snapped off large branches. The fallen fir boughs marked where she'd passed.

We stopped halfway up the mountain when we noticed no more fallen trees. Even the broken branches were smaller and fewer. The Bone Eater must have changed back to Daphne Dogwood somewhere around here. We walked a few more strides, watching for signs of the Bone Eater's trail, but all I could find were signs of the Hairysons and Darwin. They were moving up the mountain and had stopped. I stood over a patch of moist earth where I noticed deep footprints of the three sasquatches, which meant they had been standing for some time, likely getting their hair mussed up about which way to go.

Hannah sniffed the air. "I smell my parents. They're going up the mountain."

I scratched under my arm. "Something doesn't make sense, Hannah. If the Bone Eater changed back to Daphne Dogwood, Ruth would have been able to get away. Or at least, she would have been able to slow down enough that your parents would have caught up to them."

"Yes, that would make sense."

"So why haven't they?"

Hannah thought for a second. "Sour berries — we've fallen for the same trick we played on the baldfaces!"

She rushed back down the trail. I followed her, sniffing the air and looking for signs of a detour. About three hundred strides down the trail, wrapped around a branch, we found a torn strip of a red and black baldface hide, the one Ruth had been using as a sling. I pulled the hide from the branch and sniffed it. Ruth's scent was definitely on it, and so was the scent of wolf. I peeked into the woods and spotted another strip of the baldface hide.

"They definitely went this way," I said.

"Let's go," she said.

"You have to go back and get your parents. If Daphne Dogwood is strong enough to hold on to your sister, we're going to need help. I'll follow this trail and keep a watch until you join me."

"It's my sister. I should be the one who follows the trail."

"I know you, Hannah. If you see Ruth, the first thing you'll want to do is charge in and save her. We don't know anything about Daphne Dogwood's lair or about her. You make one mistake and you open yourself up to a bite — who knows what will happen?"

"I won't attack. I promise."

I shook my head. "Do you remember when my dad fell off the rock ledge and how hard I fought you to get to him? I know you'd go after your sister, because it's exactly what I'd do."

Hannah said nothing for several breaths. Then she sighed. "Okay, but if you see any sign that Ruth is going to be eaten, you won't wait, right?"

I plucked a hair from my chest. "I Sasquatch Swear that if it looks like the Bone Eater is going to hurt your sister in any way, I will step in and stop her."

She took the hair from me and nodded. A Sasquatch Swear was the strongest of all promises. The plucking of my own hair showed my determination. No sasquatch parted with their hair unless they were serious. She nodded and left.

I followed the new trail, but the further I went, the more questions popped into my head. Why hadn't Ruth kicked up more of a fuss? I hoped it might have been from the shock of seeing the change, but I feared she didn't do anything because the Bone Eater had eaten her. I yanked the hair-ible thought out of my head and tossed it away.

The sun was at its highest point in the sky and I still hadn't found the pair. I started to wonder if this was another false trail. I was about to turn around when a scent greeted my nose. Ruth. The faint smell of wolf and sasquatch also hung in the air. Ducking low, I crept through the trees toward a plateau. Then I saw it: a cave. Outside the mouth of the cave were a rock bench and the scattered bones of smaller animals. This had to be the Bone Eater's lair.

As I moved closer, I spotted Ruth sitting against the wall inside the cave. Her arm was in the tattered red and black sling and her eyes were shut, but I could see her hairy chest rising and falling. The Bone Eater must have knocked her out and carried her through the woods, which might have been why Ruth didn't fight. I took another step, but froze. A tall figure emerged from deep inside the cave.

Hairy armpits! The black-haired Daphne dwarfed even Hannah Hairyson, who was the tallest in our tribe. She bent down, blocking my view of Ruth. I slipped to the side to get a better look, but by the time I reached my new position, Daphne had slipped back inside the cave.

I searched the ground for a rock I could use as a weapon. I might be able to knock out Daphne with a lucky throw, but I couldn't find a rock large enough. Instead, I snapped off a branch from a nearby tree. The crack echoed through the woods. I ducked behind the tree and watched the mouth of the cave. Daphne stepped out, sniffed the air and looked in my direction. She bared her teeth and then charged.

CHAPTER THIRTEEN

There was nowhere I could run or hide. The only thing I could do was stand and fight. I stripped the spiky branches from the thick limb, the pine needles digging into the palm of my hand. Daphne had already covered half the distance between us. My hands shook and I quickly realized I was doomed if I didn't move. I dropped the branch and climbed up the tree. I had reached the lowest branches when the entire tree shook. I dug my toes into the wood. The scent of sasquatch and wolf wafted up. I hugged the tree and hung on for my hairy life.

"Get down!" roared Daphne.

The tree shook so hard that I felt like I was caught in a spring storm. I clenched my teeth and dug my fingers into the trunk.

"Now," she ordered.

I finally looked down. She gripped both sides of the trunk with her massive hands and shook the tree as easily as a cougar cub batted around a woodrat. Her mussed black hair looked more like a nest of snakes hissing at me. If she kept shaking the tree, I was sure to fall.

Then an idea struck. I let go of the tree and crashed into her body, knocking her to the ground. She gasped for breath as I reached around and grabbed the branch I had snapped off and pressed it down against her chest, keeping her pinned under me. As long as I kept my weight on her stomach, she couldn't buck me off. She howled and screamed as she thrashed under me. I used the branch to keep her teeth far away from me.

Her face twisted into a grimace of rage as her eyes widened and her nostrils flared. She gripped the branch with both her hands and pushed, forcing me back. Beads of sweat poured down my bare face and my hands hurt from the wood digging into them. I was losing against the beast.

"Stop that!" Ruth cried from behind us. "She's not a danger to you."

Daphne stopped struggling, but I kept the branch between us as I glanced back at Ruth, who was now standing a few strides away.

"What are you talking about? This is the Bone Eater," I said.

"No, she's not. She's Daphne Dogwood," she said.

"Hairy armpits, did you hit your head on a low-hanging branch? She was the one who grabbed you."

"I rescued her," Daphne said. "I saved her from your kind, balding face."

Ruth shook her head. "No, his face might be bare, but he's a sasquatch just like us. It's a long story, Daphne, but if you sniff him, you'll know he's just like you."

"We're nothing alike," I said. "Ruth, you saw her change, didn't you?"

She pulled me off. "Don't hurt her."

"You're helping the monster of the mountains? Why?"

"Get off her, Barnabas," she said.

I hesitated.

"Now!"

Finally, I rolled off her but I kept the branch at the ready. Daphne climbed to her feet.

"Are you all right?" Ruth asked.

"I think so," I said.

"I wasn't talking to you. Daphne, did he hurt you?"

"A little bit," she said, brushing the brambles from her hair as she glared at me.

"This is Barnabas Bigfoot. He was scared. He won't hurt you again. Just stand over there while I talk to him."

Daphne moved away from me, hiding behind a tree and watching me. I kept one eye on her. "Did she bite you?" I asked Ruth.

"No. She's not dangerous. Look at her. She's barely a sasquatchling."

Daphne peeked out from behind the tree. While she was taller than any sasquatch I had seen, her beard and moustache hadn't fully grown, a sign that a sasquatch was still very young. When Lysander the Lycanthrope said he had bitten a member of the tribe, I had always imagined a grown-up, not a sasquatchling.

"She's so young," I said.

Ruth nodded. "Come on. Let's go to Daphne's cave. I can explain."

She led us to the plateau. Daphne kept her distance and eyed me shyly, like a sasquatchling around strangers. I stepped around the small animal bones and looked in the cave. More animal bones surrounded a bedrock Daphne had set up for sleeping. She may have been a sasquatchling, but she had a gruesome appetite.

Ruth told me Daphne knew little of what had happened to her, but Ruth was able to piece together my story with what Daphne remembered: "Barnabas, your friend, Lysander went into a cave when the moon was full. The sasquatches blocked off the entrance with boulders. They left him food to eat, feeding him through an opening between rocks that was only small enough for food to be passed through, but he refused to eat the vegetables and berries they offered. They refused to give him animals. Every night, he let out hair-ible howls of hunger. The sasquatchlings heard the howls and wanted to know what caused them.

Daphne said the parents told the young ones stories of a creature called the Bone Eater, claiming he ate the bones of sasquatches. Daphne heard the howls and wanted to see the creature for herself. But she picked the last night of the full moon, when Lysander was the hungriest. She stuck her hand in the cave and he bit her wrist, thinking it was — at long last — his meat meal."

"Lysander said he left after he bit a sasquatch," I said. "He said the creature he created was terrifying. A monster."

"No. Daphne was so ashamed she'd gone against her parents she didn't tell anyone about what happened. Then, when the next full moon rose, she changed into the creature we saw last night. She was so scared she ran to her parents, but she came across some sasquatch-lings who thought she was the Bone Eater from the stories. They screamed and fled. Daphne tried to follow, but the whole tribe ran away. She could find neither hide nor hair of them. She searched for them every day, but they had hidden themselves too well. She never gave up looking, not even when she was the Bone Eater."

"That's not possible," I argued. "When Lysander turned into the wolf, he didn't know who he was or who I was. All he wanted to do was eat Hannah and me. If Daphne became like him, she'd have the same hunger for meat."

Ruth nodded. "She does eat meat, but she only hunts animals that are old. No cubs or calves."

"Did you see all the bones at her cave?"

"She saved me from the baldfaces."

"She took you so she could eat you," I whispered, glancing back at Daphne behind the tree. "The sunrise saved you, Ruth."

She shook her head. "She's not dangerous. She's scared and lonely."

"She didn't seem scared when she threw those trees at us last night," I said.

"She saw I was in trouble, just like she saw me taken to the first baldface camp. She rescued me twice."

"She might be a sasquatchling now, but don't let that fool you. When she turns, she'll become the monster of the mountains."

"I'm not a monster!" Daphne shouted.

Ruth rushed to her side and stroked her arm. "Groom your hair. He didn't mean what he said. It's all right. Take a deep breath."

"He's mean. I don't like him."

Ruth took the sasquatchling by the hand and led her toward me. "He's really nice. He's sorry for what he said. Aren't you, Barnabas?"

"Hairy armpits. You want me to apologize?"

Daphne hid behind Ruth, who glared at me. "Yes. Now."

"Fine, fine. I'm sorry if her feelings were hurt by me calling her a monster."

"You're short a few hairs on that apology. Do it again. With feeling."

I peered at Daphne. "I'm sorry for anything I said that might have upset you. That better?"

"Yes."

The monster of the mountains stuck her tongue out at me.

"Hey, did you see that?" I said. "She just — "

"Barnabas, let's not start anything else," Ruth said, leading her to the stone bench and starting to pick the brambles out of her hair.

"What do you expect us to do now?" I asked. "We can't just sit here and braid each other's hair until night when she'll turn . . . when she'll develop a temper."

She groomed Daphne's hair. "You'll see that I'm right."

"Just a sunset ago, you didn't even believe me that a sasquatch could turn into a mon . . . into the Bone Eater."

"I was wrong," she said. "But now *you* have to believe *me*."

I said nothing. The silence between us was like a spider line: thin and tense.

Ruth finally looked away and tried to lighten the mood. "What do you want to do, Daphne?"

She clapped her hands. "Can we play flying leaves?"

Ruth smiled. "Sure, but you'll have to explain how to play that game. I'm afraid I haven't heard of it."

"It's simple. Let me show you." She scrambled around the rocky surface, moving aside a large bear skull and rooting under a rib cage until she found a couple of leaves. She handed one to the Hairyson sister.

"What do I do with it?"

"Hold it up like this." She tilted her head back and held the leaf over her face, then she dropped it toward her mouth and huffed and puffed, blowing the leaf, trying to keep it afloat. "The . . . phoo . . . sasquatchling . . . phooooo . . . who can keep . . . phooooo . . . the leaf flying . . . phoo . . . the . . . phoo . . . longest . . . . phoooooo . . . . wins." She caught the leaf.

Ruth laughed and clapped her hands, then played with the sasquatchling. Daphne's chest hair curled into ringlets, a sasquatch sign of joy.

As I watched the pair play, I could see how Ruth was fooled into thinking Daphne was harmless. She had seen the change from monster to sasquatchling. I had seen the change from baldface friend to starving wolf. I wasn't about to put Ruth at risk. If she wouldn't listen to me, maybe she'd listen to her family.

I caught the flying leaf before Ruth could blow it up one more time. Daphne glared at me, folding her arms over her black-haired chest.

"It's not safe here. The baldfaces are going to be hunting for her the same way she hunted us. We have to get as far away from them as we can. For Daphne's sake."

"She can protect us from the baldfaces, Barnabas. You saw what she did back at their camp."

I nodded. "But that's only for one more night. The full moon ends after tonight and then she'll be just like us. They'll keep coming after us."

"He's scaring me," Daphne said.

Ruth shook her head. "Groom your hair. I won't let anything happen to you, but Barnabas is right. We have to leave. The baldfaces are stubborn hunters. We have to leave."

"Fine," she said. "I trust you." She clutched Ruth's hand.

"Hannah and your parents are on their way. Let's meet them and find a better place to hide."

We set off from the plateau and trekked through the woods to meet up with the rest of our group. I looked back at the bones littering the ground, then up at the sun in the sky and bit my bottom lip. Time was running out.

Chapter Fourteen

W e met up with Hannah and her parents near the point where I picked up the first strip of baldface hide. Juniper Hairyson hugged her daughter while Hemlock Hairyson ruffled her hair. Standing back from the reunion, Darwin eyed Daphne suspiciously.

"Who is she?" he asked.

"She's the Bone Eater," I said.

Ruth cut in, "But she's not dangerous."

The Hairysons and Darwin looked at us sideways, as if we were sasquatchlings caught in a hairy lie.

"There's no way that scrawny sasquatch is the Bone Eater," Darwin said.

Juniper Hairyson agreed. "How did you escape from the monster of the mountain?"

Daphne slunk behind Ruth. "I'm scared."

"We're telling the truth. Daphne's the Bone Eater," I said.

"Bald patch," Darwin said. "She doesn't look anything like the creature I saw last night."

I shook my head. "She can only turn when there's a full moon."

"Barnabas, this is no time to yank our hair," Hemlock Hairyson said.

"We're telling the truth," Hannah said. "She's the Bone Eater."

Ruth said, "Her name is Daphne."

"Groom your hair," Juniper Hairyson said. "Let's get a better look at this furball."

Daphne hid behind Ruth.

"I won't hurt you. I just want to take out some of the knots in your hair." Juniper Hairyson's voice was soft and soothing.

She stepped out from behind Ruth and moved toward Juniper Hairyson, who groomed the hair away from the sasquatchling's ears.

"What a pretty furball you are. When was the last time you ate?" she asked.

"Yesterday. I can't remember what, though."

The image of the animal bones at her camp jumped to my mind.

Juniper Hairyson stroked Daphne's head of thick black hair.

"You're brave for staying in the woods by yourself," she said, looking at Daphne's ear, which was chewed up.

"Not always. I don't like thunderstorms. They make my hair stand up."

"Me too," Ruth said.

Juniper Hairyson asked, "Furball, how did you hurt your ear?"

Daphne pulled away. "A grizzly bear bit it."

Hemlock Hairyson raised an eyebrow at his mate. Juniper Hairyson shrugged and stroked Daphne's hair.

"Tell the truth."

"I am."

Hemlock Hairyson coughed. "No sasquatch can take on a grizzly bear alone and live, let alone a sasquatchling. How did you survive?"

"She ate it," I said, recalling the bear skull at the cave.

Daphne said. "I didn't want to."

"Yes, you couldn't help yourself," I said.

"Stuff a hairball in it," Ruth said.

"Why are you helping her?" I said. "She can wipe us all out."

144

"You don't know her!"

Daphne began to cry. "I don't like it when there's yelling."

Juniper Hairyson smoothed the black hair back over the chewed ear. "Shh, shh, groom your hair. It's all right. Stop scaring her, Barnabas."

Hannah backed me up. "Listen to us. She is the Bone Eater."

Her father rose to his full height. "Enough of this hairy-brained nonsense. It's plain as the eyebrows on her face that Daphne is a sasquatchling and not the monster we saw last night. The one thing we do know is that beast is still around. Ruth, where did you see it last?"

She shrugged. "I don't know, Dad. I passed out when it grabbed me. When I woke up, Daphne was taking care of me."

"She's lying," Hannah said.

"Why are you doing this, Ruth?" I asked.

"I don't know what they're talking about."

Darwin cut in. "Bald patch. The more time we waste talking, the more time it gives the baldfaces or the Bone Eater to find us. We have to get out of here."

Hemlock Hairyson nodded. "He's right. We have to get back to the tribe."

Juniper Hairyson nuzzled her nose into Daphne's belly, making the sasquatchling giggle with glee.

I glanced at the sun, which was past its highest point and making its way down. There wasn't enough time to convince everyone of the truth about Daphne. Ruth wasn't going to leave her new friend, and now neither were the Hairysons. They saw Daphne as a cute young sasquatchling who needed our help. Even Darwin was taken with Daphne, mussing her hair and pretending the wind did it.

Then the hairy strand of an idea sprouted: we didn't have to run away from Daphne if we found a place to put her during the change — a place that would keep her and our group safe. I knew the exact place: the perma-ice cage at the baldface camp where we found Ruth. The only thing that had survived the Bone Eater's attack. I only hoped we could get there in time.

"Daphne, you know these woods better than any of us," I said. "Do you remember where you first saw Ruth?"

She nodded. "The balding faces caught her. They were in a camp."

"We call them baldfaces," Hannah said.

"Is there a way you can lead us back there?" I asked.

"That's a very bad place."

I nodded. "Yes, but we have to go there as fast as we can. Before night falls. Can you get us there?"

"Why?"

"What do you need there?" Ruth asked, her neck hair crinkling, a sasquatch sign of suspicion.

Darwin cocked his head to the side, while Hemlock Hairyson made googly eyes at Daphne.

I couldn't tell the whole truth. "The baldfaces are looking all over the valley for us. The last place they'd look for us is where they brought Ruth. They'd only go back to the camp if they caught one of us."

Hannah shook her head. "We can't be sure the baldfaces won't be there."

Her parents agreed. Juniper Hairyson said, "We would be walking right into their hands."

Darwin came to my defence. "Barnabas is right. If the Bone Eater didn't send them running from the mountains, then they won't leave the valley until they catch us. I don't think they'd go back to their camp empty handed."

Ruth shook her head. "And if Barnabas is wrong?

"There won't be any baldfaces at the camp," I said. "The one called Perkins wants his reward. You remember him talking about that, don't you Juniper Hairyson?"

She nodded. "He bragged about it all the time he held us."

"Still a big risk," Ruth said.

"Well, we can't just stay out here in the open," Darwin shot back.

"The baldfaces will find us if we don't do something soon," Daphne said.

"Daphne, can you take us to the camp?" I asked.

"All right," she finally said. "It's a long walk."

"Then we'd better hurry," I said, glancing at the sun.

Daphne headed down the slope and Hannah and her parents followed. Darwin was close on their heels.

Ruth lingered behind, pulling me close. "If this is a trick to abandon her, you'd better come clean now."

I shook my head. "I promise the last thing I want to do is leave her."

She adjusted the sling and grunted. "I'll make sure of that." Then she headed after the others.

We raced against the sun to get to the bald-face camp. Thanks to the false trail Hannah and I had created for the baldfaces to follow, we spotted no sign or scent of them. At least one hair of my plan was in place. We neared the valley. Now there were many baldfaces around the machines. Their hides were ripped and the hunters seemed bloodied and bruised. Darwin dropped back and walked beside me.

"What happened to them?" he asked.

I guessed they had met the creature in the cavern. "Looks like they ran into trouble."

Darwin raised a black eyebrow at me. "What did you and Hannah do?"

"Don't lose your hair. Let's keep going."

I jogged ahead to catch up with the others. We moved away from the clearing, careful not to leave any traces of our passing. I sniffed the air, but smelled only the baldfaces in the clearing behind us. If the hunters were looking for us, they weren't looking in this direction, which struck me as a good sign that the bald-face camp was going to be empty. I put my head down and pushed through the thick brush, following Daphne and the rest of our group. The day wore on like a slug crawling across a rock.

After countless breaths, I glanced back for Darwin, but saw no sign of him. He was gone. I waited for a few breaths. Still no sign of him. He was a strong runner, so I couldn't believe we had left him that far behind. Something had happened to him. I sniffed the air. The scent of baldface, but very faint.

I doubled backed along the trail. After a few dozen strides, I picked up the odour of my marking against the tree near the pit-trap and slowed down. A few strides ahead, the trap had been tripped. I crept closer and spotted Darwin below. He looked like a sad squirrel begging for nuts.

"What are you doing here?" I asked.

"I thought I smelled a sasquatch. I thought someone from the tribe might be near. I went to check and I fell in this hole."

His explanation was a few strands short of a full head of hair. "You expect me to believe you? What were you really doing?"

"I swear I thought I smelled a sasquatch," he said, but he refused to look into my eyes. "Now get me out!"

I suspected he was running away from us. I wanted to leave him in the trap to teach him a lesson, but I also didn't want him attracting the baldfaces. I reached over the edge and grabbed his hand. He scrambled out of the hole.

"You go ahead," he said. "I'll catch up."

I shook my head. "Stay with the group. Go." I pushed him forward and jogged behind him, making sure he didn't have another change of heart. We picked up the pace and ran through the woods until we caught up with the back of the group, then we slowed down. I caught up to Hannah.

"Keep an eye on Darwin," I whispered.

She nodded, falling back. I looked up at the sky. The sun was dipping behind the mountain. Hairy armpits; we were going to lose the race.

I trotted to the head of the group and tapped Daphne on the arm.

"Are we going to get to the camp soon?" I asked.

"Almost."

I glanced at the darkening sky. "Then for fun, we should run. See if you can beat me there."

I waved for the others to pick up the pace as I ran through the woods. Daphne easily outpaced me, leading us through the thick brush as we ran in the shadow of the mountain. I kept my head low and forged ahead, hoping to get to the camp in time.

The sun started to set as we arrived in familiar terrain. The rotting lilac and smoke smell lingered in the air and I spotted the debris of the baldface camp. Daphne slowed down, sniffing the air. I glanced at the dark camp. No light or fires, but I had to be sure. I moved along the edge of the wreckage, sniffing the air. The scent of rotting lilacs was stale. Nothing fresh. In the middle of the wreckage was the perma-ice cage. If only we had enough time to put Daphne inside. The others arrived at the camp. She wrapped her arms around Ruth, who winced and pulled back, cradling her broken arm.

"You did great, Daphne," Ruth said.

"Yes. Thank you. We'll be safe here tonight," I said.

The Hairysons gasped for air and plopped on the ground. Hemlock Hairyson whined, "My hair's too grey for all this running around."

"Me too," Juniper Hairyson gasped as she leaned against him. Hannah scanned the camp. Darwin glanced at Daphne, then looked back the way we had come. He fidgeted from one foot to the other.

"Don't worry, Darwin," Ruth said. "You're safe."

"Sure, sure," he said, his voice high and strained.

Hannah chewed her rat-tail of hair. "You sure about that, sister?"

"Yes," she said. "You have to trust me."

I glanced at the sky, which was darkening now that the sun was setting. Daphne seemed to twitch her shoulder and her beard looked a little longer than before.

"Ruth, look at her. The change is starting. We have to do something."

"No. She rescued me from that awful bald-face," she said, pushing Daphne behind with her good arm. "We're not leaving my friend."

"I'm scared," Daphne said.

"Furball, is something wrong?" Juniper Hairyson asked.

"Please get back," Hannah said. "It's not safe."

Hemlock Hairyson pulled his mate back. "What's happening to Daphne?"

Ruth barked, "Nothing."

"Too late for us to run away from her," I said, "but there's something we can do. We can put her in the baldface cage. When she changes, she won't be able to hurt anyone."

"Why would you do that?" Darwin asked.

Hannah ignored him. "Hold her in. Sweet cherries, that's a good idea."

"No! She's just a sasquatchl — "

Hannah cut her sister off, "Ruth, I saw a creature just like her turn into a monster. He nearly killed Barnabas and me. We can't take any chances!"

"She's my friend."

"Ruth!" I yelled. "You're putting us all in danger!"

Daphne shrunk behind her. "Tell them to stop shouting. I don't like loud noises."

"No one comes near her," she said, straightening to her full height. Behind her, Daphne's hair seemed to grow shaggier and she let out a low growl as her bones cracked and she grew a head taller.

Darwin stepped back, "Bald patch! You weren't lying. She is the Bone Eater!"

"She's not dangerous," Ruth said.

Juniper Hairyson yelled, "Get away from her, Ruth!"

Hemlock Hairyson shook his head. "This isn't possible. She's just a sasquatchling. There's no way she can be the Bone Eater."

Daphne cut him off with a bone-rattling roar that nearly blew Hemlock Hairyson over. If anyone had had doubts, they were gone now. Everyone started shouting at each other at once. The Hairysons tried to get Ruth to come to them, while Darwin yelled for someone to kill Daphne, who was howling in pain. Hannah yelled at everyone to be quiet. The last of the sunlight faded and night was upon us. The moon would appear soon enough. I stuck my fingers in my mouth and whistled sharply.

The group fell silent.

"Ruth, I know you're worried about Daphne, but I'm the tribe leader and I have to look out for all of us."

Darwin piped up. "My Dad is the tribe lead . . . " He stopped when Hannah twisted his arm hair. "Uh, never mind."

"Look around you, Ruth. The Bone Eater did this."

She shook her head. "She told me she saw the baldfaces take me and came to my rescue."

"Lysander said that when he turned he forgot who he was. All he knew was a great hunger. He would do anything to feed."

"I'm not hungry," Daphne said. "I just ate."

"Barnabas, have you thought that maybe he became a savage beast because the change brought out the true nature of a baldface? You've seen what the baldfaces have done. If they want something they will do anything to get it, including destroying our mountain home. What if Lysander became a wolf, but had the hunger of a baldface?"

Hannah argued, "He wasn't like the other baldfaces."

I agreed. "He wasn't greedy."

Daphne straightened up. She now stood at least four heads taller than Ruth.

"You only knew him for a short time," Ruth argued. "You don't know what he was really like."

"You barely know her," Hannah shot back.

"If I'm right and the change brings out your true nature, Daphne's true nature is being scared, and if you force her in the cage, she'll be scared of you, and she'll attack."

Daphne growled and now stood six heads taller than me. The change was coming on fast.

Hannah snarled. "Get away from her."

"No."

I stepped forward. "Ruth, I want to protect all of us, even Daphne. If you're right about her, you're putting us all in hairy danger: Me, your sister, your parents."

"Don't forget me," Darwin added.

"All I want is for her to go in the cage. When she's back to Daphne, she can come out."

Ruth shook her head. She was the most stubborn sasquatch I had ever argued with, like a hair stuck in the back of my teeth. "I'm not letting you do anything to her."

Hannah said, "That's not the sasquatch way. You have to put the tribe before yourself."

"I'm putting Daphne before myself," Ruth argued.

The monster of the mountains grew another head taller.

"Groom your hair," I said. "If this is about doing what is right for the tribe, then the decision doesn't belong to us. It belongs to her. Daphne, what do you want to do?"

She stepped out from behind Ruth. Her teeth seemed longer and sharper. "I want to be with the tribe."

"We want you to be with us too, but we have to know that we'll be safe."

Ruth argued, "I told you she won't hurt anyone."

"But we have to be sure," I said.

Daphne nodded. "You promise you won't run away like the others?"

I yanked a hair from my chest. "I Sasquatch Swear we will stand by your side no matter what happens." I walked toward her and handed her the strand.

She nodded. "I'll do it."

I smiled, then I led her to the cage. "Everyone, search the debris for the key to the cage."

"What's a key?" Hemlock Hairyson asked.

"Hannah, do you remember the key from the cage Mr. Roland put you in? The flat thing that looked like a silver leaf."

She nodded. She sifted through the wreckage around the perma-ice cage. Darwin opened the cage door, glanced inside, then moved away. Daphne and Ruth walked hand-in-hand toward the cage. Daphne was now at least ten heads taller, but she hunched her shoulders like a sasquatchling about to take her first dip in the lake. Ruth nuzzled her nose into Daphne's armpit, letting her know she was on her side.

"Groom your hair, Daphne. I won't leave you."

"Yuck. Smells funny in there."

"You won't be inside for long," I said. "Just until after the moon sets."

She hesitated.

Ruth adjusted her sling. "You're the bravest sasquatch I've ever met. I know you can do this."

Daphne cracked a smile, revealing her long fangs. Then she stepped into the cage. I closed the door behind her and pushed my back against the smooth surface. "Hairy armpits! Hurry up and find the key. The moon is rising."

Hannah sifted through the twisted metal rubble beside her parents, who kept holding up random pieces of metal and asking if they were the key. Daphne let out a strangled growl, which sounded like Lysander just before *the change*. I wasn't going to be able to hold the door on my own. I needed help.

"Darwin, forget the key. Come here and help me hold the door," I ordered. "Darwin? Darwin!" No sign of him. He had fled again. Coward.

Ruth moved to block the door. "Do what you have to. I'll hold the door."

She moved into my place, giving me the chance to search the ground. There was too much debris to find the key. Instead I found a piece of metal bar. I wedged the long metal piece under the bottom lip of the door, jamming the bar as deep into the ground as possible, hoping this would hold the door shut.

"I'm scared," Daphne said. "I want out." She started to push on the door. The bar bent, but held.

"Not yet," I said, pushing the bar further into the dirt.

"She's scared, Barnabas. Let her out," Ruth said.

"No. She has to stay in the cage," I shouted. "She can't leave!"

A booming voice shouted across the clearing. "See! I was right." Even in the darkness I recognized the voice: Dogger Dogwood.

CHAPTER FIFTEEN

Dogger Dogwood stepped from the woods along with four members of the tribe. I heard the telltale wheezing of Lorcan Longfoot and spotted the brilliant white fur of Yolanda Yeti. The other two had to be Delilah and Deacon Dogwood.

"He is a baldface trying to capture sasquatches," Dogger Dogwood said. "He's working with the Hairysons and he has thrown my son in that giant cage. Let Darwin out!"

"That's not him," Juniper Hairyson said.

"I can tell the smell of a Dogwood anywhere," he said. "And that's a Dogwood in there."

Daphne clutched her stomach and let out a deep growl, then collapsed to the ground.

"She's hurt," Ruth said.

I pushed my back against the door to keep her from escaping. "I've seen this before. It's part of *the change*."

Above us the full moon had risen and now cast its pale light on the camp. The Hairysons and Hannah backed away from the advancing sasquatches, led by Dogger Dogwood. Beside him, Deacon rubbed his black-haired hands together.

"I told you this is where they'd take Darwin, Dad."

"Yes, son. You did well. Now stuff a hairball in it."

Yolanda Yeti scanned the debris. "Where are the baldfaces, Deacon? I don't see or smell them here."

The sasquatches were armed with branches and stones. This was a rescue mission, but they were about to rescue the wrong sasquatch.

"Let my son out of there!" Dogger Dogwood ordered.

Hannah shouted, "He's not in the cage."

"Where is Darwin?" Ruth whispered to me.

"He's shown his true Dogwood colours," I said. "He ran away."

Daphne let out a high-pitched howl. Her curled-up form now filled the bottom of the cage. She was massive.

"Darwin!" Dogger Dogwood yelled. "Son! I'm here to save you. Sister, clear those traitors out of the way."

Delilah Dogwood yelled, "Attack!"

They clashed atop the wreckage. Hemlock Hairyson fell under Yolanda Yeti's weight, while Juniper Hairyson held her own against Lorcan Longfoot. Deacon and Hannah were evenly matched as well, but Delilah Dogwood kicked Hannah's leg and swung the advantage to her nephew. Then she waved her brother over. Dogger Dogwood ran through the rubble and came whisker to stubble with me.

"Get out of the way. I'm here for my son."

"That's not Darwin," I said.

"I'll have you out in a few breaths," he yelled at the cage.

"Dad! Dad!" Darwin shouted from the far end of the clearing. "Get out of here!"

"Darwin? If you're here, then who in the bald patch is in there?" Dogger Dogwood asked.

"You have to go." Darwin rushed around the cage, waving at his father and aunt. "It's not safe here."

Dogger Dogwood's eyebrows knitted together in confusion. "Who's in the cage?"

Daphne howled in answer.

"She's hurt." Ruth tried to open the door, but I refused to budge.

"I want to know who you've taken," Dogger Dogwood said.

"Forget that," Darwin said. "We have to go now!"

"Mind your place," Delilah Dogwood barked. "Your father is the tribe leader now."

I shook my head. "*I* am."

He scowled at me. "With the last of the Bigfoots turning out to be a baldface, the tribe decided to choose a true sasquatch. Now step out of the way."

"No, Dad! Don't."

"Why?"

In answer, Daphne let out an ear-splitting roar. *The change* was complete. The Bone Eater rose up, bashing her head against the top of the cage. Even stooped in the cage, she looked gigantic. She roared at us. I stood my ground, pushing my back against the door. The Dogwoods scurried back while the battle behind them came to a stop and all eyes fell on the Bone Eater.

"Skunky tail!" Dogger Dogwood said. "What is that?!"

Delilah Dogwood pulled her brother and nephew behind her. "The legends are true."

Yolanda Yeti and Lorcan Longfoot let the Hairysons get up while Deacon gaped slack-jawed at the massive monster of the mountains. Hannah shoved him off her and rolled on to her feet.

Ruth banged on the perma-ice wall with her good arm and shouted, "Daphne, it's okay. You're safe. You don't have to be scared."

The Bone Eater wasn't listening to her. She bashed her shoulder against the side of the cage, rocking it to one side, then smashed the other side with the other shoulder, shaking the ground beneath our feet. The cage walls were holding, but it wouldn't be long before she turned her fury on the door.

"Get out of here," I said. "I don't know how much longer we can hold this door shut."

"Don't," Ruth said. "She's scared that we'll leave her."

The Bone Eater slammed her fist against the door and nearly knocked us to the ground. The bar still held and the door remained closed.

Ruth pleaded, "Don't take another step. You're making it worse."

Dogger Dogwood's hair stood on end as he waved at the others to back up. "We must flee."

"No!" Ruth yelled.

"Flee," I said. "She's a monster! Look at her."

Daphne bared her yellow fangs at us and struck the door again. The metal bar bent from the force. I shifted my weight to hold the door shut.

"She's just scared," Ruth argued.

The Hairysons stood their ground, refusing to leave their daughter, but Dogger Dogwood's group backed away toward the trees. They were halfway there when Darwin waved at them to stop, his black hair standing up like porcupine quills. "Look out!"

The woods erupted with shouts and bright lights shone in our eyes. A sleeping arrow plinked off the perma-ice wall next to my head. Lorcan Longfoot yelped and clutched his chest, then flopped to the ground. Sasquatches ran every which way and the baldfaces emerged from the woods, armed with their hiccupping rifles.

Delilah Dogwood let out a fierce howl as her brother hid behind her. Darwin ran toward us. Deacon scrambled after him, but yelped and grabbed his butt where a sleeping arrow had struck him. He stumbled two steps before falling to the rubble.

"Get away!" I yelled at the Hairysons. "I can't hold the door any longer."

The Bone Eater roared. Ruth pleaded, "Groom your hair, Daphne."

Hemlock Hairyson stiffened and fell, a sleeping arrow sticking out of his neck. Juniper Hairyson rushed to his side, trying to shake him awake. A sleeping arrow hit her in the shoulder. She clutched the arrow, then fainted beside her mate. Hannah dodged the flying weapons, running left and right, hopping over the debris, lifting a large piece of metal to use as a shield. The sleeping arrows plinked off harmlessly.

Yolanda Yeti roared and slung her thick club at her attackers. The weapon spun through the air and connected with two of the baldfaces, knocking them down. She scrambled away as a flurry of sleeping arrows whizzed past her. She ran to the cage along with Dogger and Delilah Dogwood. Darwin fell by the cage and curled up in a ball and went to sleep.

Hannah reached the woods and disappeared, followed by four baldfaces. The Bone Eater pounded on the door. Ruth grabbed my arm. "The baldfaces have us surrounded. Daphne can save us."

I shook my head. "She'll eat us."

"Trust me!"

The monster of the mountains roared again, pushing against the door. The metal bar bent more, but now Yolanda Yeti was helping us hold it closed. Delilah Dogwood scooped up a rock and hurled it at the baldfaces, knocking down one of the hunters.

Behind the hunter, Perkins raised his rifle and fired. Delilah Dogwood yelped as a sleeping arrow struck her dead-centre in the chest. She turned to me, her eyes rolling up into her head as she flopped to the ground. Dogger Dogwood grabbed Ruth and used her as a shield.

The Bone Eater smashed the door repeatedly. Yolanda Yeti and I forced our full weight against the door, but then she let out a yip.

"Yolanda Yeti?" I asked.

She slumped to the ground. A sleeping arrow stuck out of her neck.

Dogger Dogwood yelled, "Take her! Leave me alone."

A sleeping arrow struck Ruth. She went limp in Dogger Dogwood's arms, but he refused to let her go. The baldfaces closed in around us. The Bone Eater pounded her giant fists against the door. This was like deciding whether I wanted to be eaten by a cougar or mauled by a grizzly bear. The beams of light settled on the cage. I could hear the baldfaces crunching through the debris. Dogger Dogwood was no help, clutching the sleeping Ruth and begging for his life. "Please take the others. Just leave me."

Perkins barked, "Put them to sleep. All of them."

I had no other choice. I reached down, pulled out the metal bar and swung the door open, pushing Dogger Dogwood and Ruth to one side. The Bone Eater burst out of the cage and roared. A flurry of sleep arrows flew at her, but they bounced harmlessly off her thick hairy hide.

"Run!" a baldface shouted.

The Bone Eater lumbered past me and picked up a panel of wood. She hurled the flat wall at the baldfaces. The light sticks fell to the ground, casting their beams along the wreckage and the sleeping forms of my tribe members. The baldfaces ran into the woods, fleeing for their lives. She hurled more debris at them, knocking a few to the ground. They didn't get back up. Ruth was right. Daphne was no monster. She was saving us. I took the metal bar that had once held the cage door shut and helped her chase off the baldfaces.

The baldfaces dropped their rifles and ran through the woods like scared deer. One didn't look where he was going and ran into a low-hanging branch, which knocked him senseless. Another baldface scrambled up a tree to hide. Daphne toppled both the tree and baldface over. I liked this new game of Baldface Chase.

The woods were filled with the screams of baldfaces as they ran for their lives. Every now and then I heard Daphne's howl and the crash of a tree. She was about thirty strides away from me when I noticed a baldface crouched by a tree. In the pale moonlight, I could make out the lanky form of Perkins. He held up the electric prod. Blue sparks danced on the end.

In the next breath, everything moved slowly, as if I were under the lake and swimming against the current. Perkins rose to his feet, jabbing the prod into Daphne's thigh. She let out a high-pitched yelp. He stabbed her in the stomach and lightning danced from the stick to her body. She howled in pain. He jabbed her in the stomach and the chest as she sank to the ground. He wouldn't stop attacking her with the stick. She curled up in a ball and whimpered as he continued poking her.

I charged at Perkins and leapt in the air, slamming into him. A bright flash lit up in my face and I felt searing heat against my cheek. We both landed on the ground, but Perkins rolled to his feet quickly and pointed the prod at me.

"Almost, but I've hunted more dangerous game than you."

"Don't forget me!" cried Hannah, as she leapt down from a tree and crashed into him.

He crumpled to the ground, unconscious. The prod fell out of his hand. I picked it up and hurled the stick at a nearby pine tree with all my might. The prod cracked in two pieces and fell to the ground.

Hannah brushed herself off. "Are you all right?"

My face tingled and I had trouble making words with my mouth.

Daphne slowly rose to her feet. She winced as she moved, but she was all right. I nodded at her. She roared and ran into the woods to hunt the other baldfaces.

Hannah patted my shoulder. "I think we owe my sister an apology."

I smiled. "Yes, yes we do. As soon as she wakes up."

We headed back to the camp. The sleeping sasquatches were lying all over the camp along with a few baldface hunters. The wreckage looked eerie in the moonlight. A few light sticks cut across the debris, like shafts of sunlight, lighting up the damage that Daphne had done. In the middle of the hairy mess, Dogger Dogwood knelt by Darwin, gently pulling out the sleeping arrow and smoothing strands of his son's hair away from his eyes. "Wake up, son. Please, wake up."

Anger welled in me as I walked toward him. Dogger Dogwood was the true monster of the mountains. All Daphne wanted was to be a part of the tribe; Dogger Dogwood wanted to break up the tribe. I towered over him, glaring at him in silence. Then I moved away to help the others.

"They were shot with sleeping arrows," Hannah explained to Dogger Dogwood. "They'll wake up. If we're lucky, probably by the time the sun rises. Until then, we have to protect them from any baldfaces who might come to the camp."

Dogger Dogwood stroked his black neck hair. "More likely we'll have to defend ourselves against the Bone Eater."

"Did you ever wonder why the Bone Eater smelled like a Dogwood?" I shot back.

His black eyebrows knitted together in confusion. "Why?"

I was too tired to explain. Instead, I walked over to Ruth. She was breathing. Hannah helped me move her sister. Then we moved her parents closer to Ruth. There was a crack and snap to my right. Dogger Dogwood was moving his son away from us to the ground on the other side of the cage. He gathered his family members, while Hannah and I gathered Yolanda Yeti and Lorcan Longfoot and laid them beside the Hairysons.

When we were done, I walked to the edge of the clearing and listened for any sign of hunters. All I could hear were Daphne's roars and a few screams from the frightened bald-faces. I suspected they would think twice before they decided to hunt sasquatches again. I moved the sleeping baldfaces into the perma-ice cage. I started with Perkins, tossing him in the cage. Dogger Dogwood was busy tending to his sleeping family members and didn't lift a hairy finger.

"I'll help," Hannah said. "I think I knocked out most of the ones you'll find."

I shook my head. "Keep your eye on him."

She nodded. I worked through the night, trekking into the woods to fetch baldfaces back to camp. Every now and then I heard another baldface screaming. I couldn't help but smile at the thought of the scared hunters running for their lives. By the time I was finished, about a dozen hunters were in the cage. I wedged the metal bar in front of the door to keep them locked in. I hadn't heard Daphne's roars or baldface screams in quite a few breaths.

Lorcan Longfoot started to stir and Hannah rushed to his side. Dogger Dogwood slapped the faces of his family members as they began to stir. He whispered to them as they began to sit up. Meanwhile, I tried to wake Ruth, but she was dead asleep. The last to be struck with sleeping arrows, she would be out for a while; I didn't know how long. I let her sleep and went to check on her parents.

Before I took two strides, a body crashed into me. Darwin Dogwood. He straddled me and pinned me down. I looked up to see Delilah Dogwood grab Hannah. Deacon was headed to the perma-ice cage to open the door.

His father rushed to Yolanda Yeti's side and patted her face. "Wake up!"

"What happened?" she asked.

"I saved us from the baldfaces," Dogger said.

"What?" My mouth dropped open in surprise.

"If it weren't for me, we'd all be in the hands of the evil baldfaces and Barnabas Bigfoot."

"Liar!" I shouted, struggling to get up.

"Darwin and I put them in the cage. Now we need your help to get Barnabas in there as well as the Hairysons. I'll explain everything later, but right now we have to hurry."

"Don't listen to him."

He cracked a yellow smile at me. "This baldface is the last one to go in and then our tribe will be safe from them forever."

Yolanda Yeti climbed to her feet and saw the baldfaces in the cage, then she glared at me, her nostrils flaring wide open.

Hannah struggled against Delilah Dogwood, but couldn't move.

Yolanda Yeti snarled at me. "You traitor."

Suddenly the ground began to shake and there was loud crashing in the woods ahead. Yolanda Yeti froze. Dogger Dogwood crouched low. "The Bone Eater's coming back. We must flee!"

Before anyone could move, Daphne burst through the woods and roared when she saw Dogger Dogwood. He backed away from her. She charged at him, growling. The debris snapped and crunched under her massive feet.

"Monster!" Delilah Dogwood screamed. Hannah pushed her attacker to the ground and the two wrestled in the dirt.

"Dad! Get out of there!" Deacon yelled.

Dogger Dogwood rushed to his son's side by the cage. I bucked Darwin off and rolled to my feet as Daphne lumbered toward the cage. In true Dogwood form, he pulled his son in front of him as a shield. Daphne bared her giant fangs at the pair and howled. Deacon began to cry.

"Don't hurt us," Dogger Dogwood pleaded. "Please. Take the others first, but leave us."

Yolanda Yeti stiffened. "What kind of a leader are you?"

Daphne roared and began to reach out for the Dogwoods. I wanted her to crush them for what they had done to us, but something nagged at me. Grandma Bertha's saying replayed in my head: "A tree will fall, but a forest stands forever." I had no right to deliver Dogger Dogwood's punishment. For the tribe to be strong, the members had to make the decision together.

"Stop."

Daphne glanced at the sleeping Ruth, then pointed at Dogger Dogwood and roared.

"Yes, what he did was wrong. He did many things wrong, but you'd be just as wrong if you hurt him."

She hesitated, cocking her head to the right. She pointed to Ruth again. She stomped toward Dogger Dogwood, who shrunk behind his son.

"He will answer for what he did," I said.

She shook her head and roared. She wanted to deliver the punishment. She lunged for the older Dogwood, pushing Deacon aside and picking up the screaming sasquatch in her giant hands.

"Put me down!" squealed Dogger Dogwood.

Daphne roared again.

"Groom your hair," Ruth said, sitting up and cradling her broken arm. "You're yelling loud enough to wake the dead."

Daphne turned and smiled at Ruth who was climbing to her feet. The Hairysons also stirred.

"Put him down," I ordered.

She refused.

"Do what Barnabas says. He's your tribe leader."

Deacon protested. "No, the tribe picked my dad."

Daphne growled at him.

"But they can always change their minds." He closed himself inside the cage.

"Someone help me!" Dogger Dogwood yelled. "Please!"

I moved closer to Daphne, within arm's reach. Yolanda Yeti gasped. "The Bone Eater will eat you."

I ignored her. "Daphne, do you want to play flying leaves?" I asked.

She stopped, cracking a smile, revealing a bit of a snaggletooth, just like Dogger Dogwood's stray fang.

"Well, you'll have lots of sasquatches to play with, including your family." I motioned to the Dogwoods. "All of them. Dogger and Delilah Dogwood. And Darwin and Deacon. They're your family."

"Impossible," Dogger Dogwood said. "This beast isn't a Dogwood. It's not even a sasquatch."

"She's as much a sasquatch as I am," I said.

Lorcan Longfoot climbed to his feet. "It's one of the baldface lies to trick us."

Yolanda Yeti shook her head. "I'm not so sure if he is tricking us."

Juniper Hairyson leapt to my defence. "Barnabas Bigfoot has done nothing but help this tribe since he returned, Lorcan."

"A traitor's words are as light as a feather," he said. "He's up to no good."

Hemlock Hairyson rose up. "Then why are the baldfaces in the cage and not us?"

Dogger Dogwood barked, "I did that. Not him."

I shook my head. "He lies."

"Says the sasquatch freak who wants us to believe he and this monster are one of us."

Daphne growled.

"This is no sasquatch," Dogger Dogwood said. "And it most certainly isn't a Dogwood."

Ruth sighed. "Then it's the Bone Eater and you're going to be its last meal of the night."

Daphne licked her lips.

"No, no, no. Make her put me down."

"Not yet," I said. "Not until you tell everyone the truth."

"I have been as honest as my hair is long," he said.

Daphne squeezed him and opened her jaws as if to eat his head.

"Stop, stop, stop! All right! All right. I lied about Barnabas and the Hairysons."

Yolanda Yeti and Lorcan Longfoot gasped.

"Tell him how you tied us up and left us for the baldfaces," Hannah said.

"I did, I did. I'm sorry, but I wanted to protect the tribe. The Bigfoots nearly ruined us all. I was doing it for the good of the tribe."

I turned to Yolanda Yeti and Lorcan Longfoot. "Do you need to know any more?"

They shook their heads.

"Put him down, Daphne."

She growled, but reluctantly lowered him to the ground.

The Dogwoods gathered around him as he straightened up and groomed his black hair. "I have no shame for trying to save the tribe. You may have stopped these baldfaces, but there will be more. Now that they know we're here, there will be no peace in these mountains."

Yolanda Yeti stepped forward, "Sasquatches do not betray each other, Dogger. What you did was not to save the tribe. What you did was for your own hairy glory."

"We do what we must to survive, and I would rather take my chances on my own than under the leadership of this small-footed freak." He turned and walked out of the camp. His family followed. Daphne growled, but I held up my hand. "Let them go. The Dogwood clan has made their choice."

We watched in silence as they left. They reached the edge of the clearing when the first rays of the sun cut through the night. Daphne clutched her side and doubled over. Ruth rushed to her side. So did Hannah and I. The Hairysons pulled Yolanda Yeti and Lorcan Longfoot back.

The change from the monster of the mountains to Daphne was hair-ible to watch. She curled into a ball as her hair and flesh swirled like a violent stream. She moaned in pain, clutching her stomach as she shrunk before our eyes. Her bones cracked as she twisted on the ground. It was like every strand of hair had to crawl back inside her body and every bit of her flesh had to turn inside out. By the time the sun had crested over the mountain, Daphne was back to her old self.

The other sasquatches gathered around, as Ruth stroked Daphne's hair. "It's all right, Daphne. You're safe."

The sasquatchling sobbed. "No, it's not. My family, they hate me. They ran away from me."

I knelt beside her. "You're wrong. Your family is right here." I put my hand on her shoulder.

Ruth smiled. "Yes, we're here." She put her hand on Daphne's other shoulder and helped her sit up.

Hannah crouched in front of the sasquatchling. "I'd love to teach you how to play Baldface Chase, little sister."

Ruth looked to her parents. "Can we?"

Juniper Hairyson looked to her mate, who nodded. They smiled at Daphne. "What's another mouth to feed?"

Daphne beamed and threw her arms around Ruth. She wasn't going to be alone ever again.

CHAPTER SIXTEEN

We had left the baldfaces trapped in their cage and trekked back to the tribe. As Lorcan Longfoot led the way, Yolanda Yeti slowed down and walked with me for a way in silence.

Finally, she spoke. "I'm sorry I doubted you, Barnabas. I should have always known the Bigfoot clan were real sasquatches."

"It's all right," I said. "Dogger Dogwood had us all fooled."

"But that doesn't change the fact that I turned against your clan. I won't ever turn my back on you again. I Sasquatch Swear that." She plucked a hair from her chest and handed it to me.

"Thank you," I said. "That means a lot to our family."

When we found the tribe, Yolanda Yeti and Lorcan Longfoot told the story of Dogger Dogwood's betrayal. The Hairysons were welcomed back into the tribe with open arms. So was Daphne, even though the telling of her story had more than a few sasquatches casting sideways glances at the sisters.

It took the tribe members longer to accept me. My bare face and small feet had many of the sasquatches wondering if there was truth to the Dogwood accusations. To have a bare-faced leader was more than some of the sasquatches could bear. Few of the older sasquatches listened to me and the sasquatchlings fled at the sight of my bare face.

We took over Daphne's cave as a temporary den. Of course, we swept away the animal bones before any of the sasquatchlings arrived. The third night after the last full moon, the tribe gathered to talk about what to do.

First, there was the matter of my missing mother and grandparents. They should have returned long ago from scouting a new home. Yolanda Yeti wanted to send out searchers to find them, fearing that they had fallen into a crevice. We knew they had gone to the high mountains where there were no baldfaces, but that didn't mean there weren't other dangers. We agreed to look for them after we found a safe place for the tribe.

That led to the talk of where to locate our permanent home. Daphne's cave was too small for the tribe. Hannah, Ruth, and I agreed not to mention the cavern we had found because of the creature and the strange lights. The tribe agreed to head higher in the mountains to find a new cave. With the baldfaces in the valley, I knew it was important to go where no bald-faces could follow, and the best place would be higher up. But no one would even listen to me. I realized I still had to earn their respect.

I raised my hand and shouted for attention, but the sasquatches talked over me. Finally, Yolanda Yeti placed her fingers in her mouth and whistled. Everyone settled down. She nodded to me.

"I know that I don't look like you with my feet and my face. My hair will grow, but I can't do anything about my feet. All I can do is prove to you that I'm a sasquatch by my actions, and I know that the tribe comes first. If you won't listen to me as the tribe leader, then I'll step down so you can choose someone who you do want to follow."

Lorcan Longfoot yipped and nodded. So did many of the others. The Hairysons shook their heads.

Yolanda Yeti stood and addressed me. "Barnabas Bigfoot, that is a wise choice you have made. Dogger Dogwood was willing to betray the tribe members to lead us, and you would rather step down than cause a hairy tangle. To me, that is a true leader. I pick you."

Lorcan Longfoot spoke up, "But his feet are so small. What kind of leader would he be?"

"He was born with small feet," Hannah said. "He can't help that, but he acts like a tribe leader. He saved my family from the baldfaces."

Lorcan Longfoot asked, "Why would he choose to cut off his hair?"

"I told you the story. I had to blend in with the baldfaces," I explained. "So I could survive."

Winnow Willknot shook her head. "I'm just worried about how much he cares about the tribe. I'm not even sure if he's a true sasquatch."

The others muttered, some in agreement, others unsure.

I straightened to my full height. "Then pick what your heart tells you to pick. If you believe I am one of you, then let me lead you. If not, pick another. Who will stand for the tribe leader? Lorcan Longfoot, will you?"

He looked down at his feet.

"There doesn't have to be another. No other sasquatch has sacrificed so much for this tribe. You are my leader," Juniper Hairyson said, raising three of her fingers. Her mate did the same, as did the Hairyson sisters. Even Daphne raised her three fingers.

Lorcan Longfoot folded his arms over his chest. Winnow Willknot looked down at the ground. Slowly, the other sasquatches raised their hands. Not everyone agreed, but enough did. Yolanda Yeti nodded at me and grinned.

"Barnabas Bigfoot, you are now our tribe leader."

Lorcan Longfoot grumbled, "He'll be the end of us."

"Stuff a hairball in it, Lorcan," barked a voice from outside the circle. "He's more a sasquatch than you'll ever be. I watched him grow from a sasquatchling and he's a Bigfoot from chin stubble to toe hair."

Everyone turned. Gasps rippled through the group. Standing before the group were Grandma Bertha and Grandpa Benson, their hair matted and bare in some places. Everyone chattered at once as I rushed to my grandparents.

"Are you all right?" I asked.

"Nothing a few dried berries won't fix," Grandma Bertha said, placing her big hand on my shoulder and leaning against me.

"What happened?" Yolanda Yeti asked.

"We ran into a hairy tangle," Grandpa Benson answered. "Water, I need water." He lowered himself to the ground while Yolanda Yeti rushed to fetch him water.

"Where's Mom?" I asked.

"She's been taken," Grandma Bertha answered. "Barnabas, she's in danger."

"From what?"

"Hair-ible. I've never seen anything like it before. A creature rising from black waters. I'd heard legends, but never believed this monster could exist."

"What, Grandma?"

"The Beast of Skeleton Lake."

Novelist, playwright, television writer, and radio humorist, Marty Chan has been entertaining audiences across Canada for over fifteen years. His first children's novel, *The Mystery of the Frozen Brains*, won the 2005 City of Edmonton Book Prize. The sequel, *The Mystery of the Graffiti Ghoul*, won the 2008 Diamond Willow Award. His stage play, *Mom, Dad, I'm Living with a White Girl,* has been produced across Canada as well as Off Broadway in New York. Chan lives in Edmonton, Alberta.